THE SUPERNORMAL SLEUTHING SERVICE

BOOK TWO

The Sphinx's Secret

THE SUPERNORMAL SLEUTHING SERVICE

BOOK TWO
The Sphinx's Secret

Gwenda Bond & Christopher Rowe

ILLUSTRATED BY
Glenn Thomas

The Sphinx's Secret
Text copyright © 2018 by Gwenda Bond
and Christopher Rowe;
illustrations copyright © 2018 by Glenn Thomas

The text of this book is set in 13-point Hoefler Text.
Book design by Paul Zakris

Library of Congress Control Number: 2018940381

ISBN 9780062459978 (trade ed.)

18 19 20 21 22 PC/LSCH 10 9 8 7 6 5 4 3 2 1

First Edition

GREENWILLOW BOOKS

For Amanda Connor, maker of magic and friend to dragons,
and for all the other extraordinary people
who put books into the hands of children

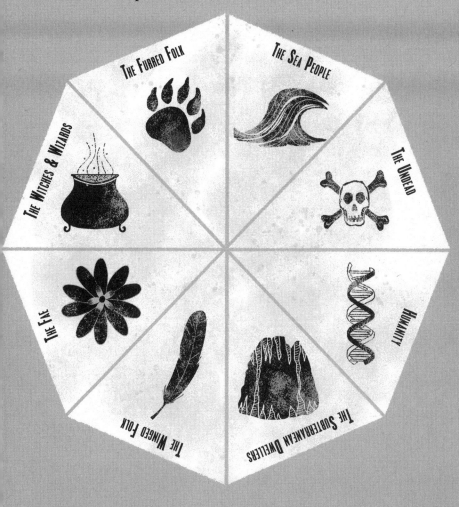

CHAPTER ONE

Thwack!

A red croquet ball flew through the air, bounced hard off the marble floor of the hotel lobby, then crashed into the closed doors of the elevator.

"Ouch!" came the elevator's muffled cry. "That better not have left a mark!"

Stephen dove, sliding across the Octagon symbol embedded in the marble and scooping the ball up in both hands.

"Got the red one!" he shouted.

Just then a monkey holding a croquet mallet landed on his shoulder, screeching in delight. It plucked the ball from Stephen's hands and was gone in an instant. A chandelier rattled as the monkey swung from it into the forest that dominated the

New Harmonia's lobby. More monkeys were visible up in the tree branches—some tossing brightly colored balls back and forth, others swinging mallets.

"Um, lost it again," Stephen said, mostly to himself, because everybody else was too busy shouting, ducking, or generally scrambling around to pay him any attention.

Ivan appeared out of the chaos. "I said from the beginning it was a bad idea to teach the monkeys to play croquet," said the boy detective, adjusting the bow tie of his neat navy suit—even though, as usual, it did not need to be adjusted.

"We were just trying to keep them out of trouble," said Stephen. "Besides, it was Sofia's idea, not mine. Where is she, anyway?"

"En garde!" Sofia's voice came from up in the trees.

"There!" said Ivan, pointing.

Sofia danced along a tree branch, twenty feet in the air, holding a croquet mallet like a fencing sword. A monkey with its own mallet skittered backward along the branch, then dropped its mallet before jumping clear.

"Look out!" shouted Stephen and Ivan together. The spinning mallet was going to land . . . smack on a high level of the long, tiered front desk, where it smashed into an inkwell. A tremendous splash of blue ink exploded outward. It coated the surface of the desk, the registration book, the desk clerk, and the towering centaur guest who had just been signing his name.

Silence fell over the lobby. Even the monkeys quieted down.

The members of the Perilous Guard who'd been chasing the monkeys stopped what they were doing and turned to stare at Ivan and Stephen. The guests who'd been scurrying for cover did the same.

The desk clerk shot the kids a panicked look, ineffectively dabbing at the centaur's face with a handkerchief. The centaur, his brown skin and white linen suit now a brilliant blue, positively glared.

"That ink is crafted especially for the hotel by the inksmith gnomes of Winnipeg," said Ivan. "Erm, it's magically indelible."

A door opened behind the registration desk, and Sofia's mother, Carmen—the Knight Diplomatis, who ran the hotel—marched out in a business suit sporting a gold name badge.

"What on earth is going on out here?" she demanded.

Uh-oh, Stephen thought. *Now we're in for it.* It would have been a great time for Ivan to break out some invisibility spray from a hidden suit pocket.

Carmen scanned the large lobby, grimacing when she saw the centaur dripping blue, before settling her gaze on Stephen and Ivan.

"Boys," Carmen said evenly, "where is my daughter?"

"I'm up here, Mom," said Sofia, nimbly jumping down from the branch where she'd been dueling to another one ten feet below. The lower branch bowed under her weight, but Sofia bent her knees with it and used it to launch herself into the air. She tucked in tight, spun in a somersault, then landed right beside Stephen. How she managed to hit the ground so silently in her heavy boots he didn't know.

"Or rather, down here," Sofia said.

Most of the people in the lobby gaped at Sofia's display of acrobatic prowess, but her mother barely seemed to notice. She had rounded the desk and was speaking to the huffing centaur in low, soothing tones. Stephen heard the words "complimentary stay" and "new suit at our expense" and "get you cleaned up somehow."

"Maybe we should head back upstairs," Stephen whispered to Ivan and Sofia.

Carmen heard him. "Maybe you should stay

exactly where you are and not move a muscle until I tell you," she said.

Too late.

"Mom!" Sofia started to protest. But Carmen held up a single finger, and Sofia gulped, swallowing whatever else she'd been about to say.

An idea that might get them out of this mess—at least the centaur part of it—occurred to Stephen, and he worked up the courage to speak. "Um, Mrs. Gutierrez," he said. "Mr., um, Centaur?"

Carmen and the centaur stopped their conversation and stared at Stephen. He rushed to finish before they could tell him to quiet down. "I know the ink is, um, indelible or whatever, but my dad and his staff in the kitchen have this special cleaning fluid. Universal something?"

"Of course!" said Ivan. "Universal Defixitive!" He smiled as if it had been his idea. "And it's rated food safe, so it shouldn't burn your skin off or anything!"

Carmen turned to the desk clerk. "Simeon, please take Master Windmane down to the kitchen and explain this . . . situation . . . to Chef Lawson. Tell him I authorized the use of the Defixitive, as I know he'll be concerned since it's so very, *very* expensive."

Stephen was pretty sure the last words were aimed at the three of them. Exactly how much did the magical cleaning fluid cost, and for that matter, how much did a linen suit for a centaur cost? He could guess the weekly allowances he, Sofia, and Ivan received wouldn't be enough to cover it.

Once the centaur had been led away, Carmen walked over to the stairwell door and opened it. She called out, "Monkeys! Back upstairs!"

With a tremendous clatter of dropped croquet balls and mallets, but uttering neither screech nor scream, the troupe of monkeys flowed down out of the trees and into the stairwell as quick as a thought. The monkeys listened to Carmen. Sometimes. No one else could begin to control them.

"I believe you three are aware the monkeys are not allowed in the lobby," said Carmen. "So, which one of you has an explanation?"

"It's not our fault they're down here." Stephen hesitated. "Not exactly."

"Sofia, is this because I told you you've been spending too much time on sword practice?"

"No," Sofia said, and even Stephen wasn't convinced. "We really were trying to help. I need better croquet opponents—"

Stephen shot Ivan a look, and they both shook their heads, affronted. But Sofia continued.

"—and we figured if the monkeys were playing croquet, they'd stay in the Village and out of your hair."

"Uh-huh," Carmen said. "But instead . . ."

"Well," Sofia said, studying the high ceiling, "before we could stop them, they stole the croquet set and made for the lobby."

"In our, erm, defense," Ivan said, "it's not as if we have anything better to do. If you would let us assist with minor investigations while my parents are working on bigger cases, then we could—"

Carmen held up a hand, and Ivan stopped talking. "It's true . . . ," she said.

But Stephen doubted she agreed the three of them should do the job of the hotel's masters of detection.

"You *don't* have anything better to do," Carmen continued. "It's your summer vacation." She paused and then waved her hand. "So, go play outside."

"We *were* outside in the Village, *playing* croquet," Sofia said. "Before."

"And we're not children," Stephen said. Carmen lifted her eyebrow. "Okay, fine, but we're not *babies*."

Ivan stepped forward. "I think the Knight Diplomatis is kicking us out of the hotel for the rest of the day."

"Finally," Carmen said, "someone understands me. Stephen, I'll let your dad know you guys are out in the city. Have fun." She paused again. "Don't even *think* about taking the monkeys. *Or* getting in trouble. *And* be back before dark." She walked away.

"As if we'd take those stinking monkeys," Sofia grumbled.

Stephen didn't think it was entirely fair to blame the monkeys for being, well, monkeys. They hadn't asked to be sent to Cindermass as a birthday gift—and Carmen hadn't been successful in convincing the dragon to let them live in his basement lair. So, they popped up in the most inconvenient places around the hotel, pretty much everywhere except the elevator, which had refused to let them aboard, declaring, "I have to draw the line somewhere, and that horde of monkeys is where. Put them back in their barrel, I say. Why should they have more freedom than one such as I?"

The elevator had a flare for the dramatic. *Actually,* Stephen thought as Ivan flung his arms out wide and smiled at him and Sofia, *everyone at the New Harmonia has a flare for the dramatic.* Stephen had discovered he sometimes did, too. Living here? Hanging out with his new friends every day—having real, good friends *to* hang out with every day? It was a dream come true. Maybe it was better. This life—being part of a secret supernormal society—was something he'd never known to dream for himself.

"The city is our oyster," Ivan declared. "And I

know exactly where we should go. Follow me."

Sofia shrugged at Stephen, who grinned back at her, and the two of them did as commanded, trailing Ivan across the lobby and through the front doors to the street outside. He seemed to be in no rush to say where they were going, though he did pause to knock on the window of Dr. Bethuselah's Fountain Pen & Inkporium and wave to the owner.

Stephen couldn't take the suspense. "So, Ivan, where *are* we going?"

Sofia appeared on Ivan's other side. "We could go watch the fae jousts in the park," she said.

"It's too hot out," Ivan said.

Stephen hadn't known about the jousts and wouldn't have minded checking them out. His mother was fae—something he'd learned when he and his dad had moved to the hotel several weeks ago. He'd been pretty freaked to find out he wasn't entirely human, but instead half fae. *And* it turned out his mother wasn't just any fae, but a princess. She'd returned from exile for Cindermass the dragon's birthday party to retake her seat on the

Octagon, the council of eight members who oversaw supernormal affairs.

Even if jousts hadn't come up yet, Stephen had been visiting his mother's new apartment in the city and learning more about the fae from her. Apparently not all of them were as awful as the first ones he'd met, who'd tried to frame him for a theft and make him and his friends their servants. No, his mother was glamorous and blue-skinned, with the same pointed ears he had. And she was kind. He still felt shy around her. Having both of his parents in the same place *also* felt like a dream come true, and another he'd never known to wish for.

"Ivan," Sofia said, and heaved a long, drawn-out sigh, "tell us where we're going."

Ivan didn't even blink. "We're going to the library, of course."

"But we could go anywhere," Sofia said. "Why—"

Stephen interrupted. "I thought the library was on the third floor?"

"Not that library," Ivan said to him. And then

to Sofia: "Stephen has never seen the Cabinet of Wonders."

"Okay, okay," Sofia said grudgingly. "The Cabinet of Wonders *is* cool."

"What is it?" Stephen asked. It did, in fact, sound cool.

"Wait until we get on the bus," Ivan said, and pushed his glasses up on his nose.

A bus pulled up at the transit sign near the corner. A normal city bus. They'd had these back in Chicago. Ivan and Sofia got on first, and Sofia gave an extra swipe of her MetroCard to cover Stephen's fare. They trundled to the back, where there were two seats and a hand strap free.

Stephen blinked as they passed a troll in a green suit reading something called the *Supernormal Times*. "Supernormals have their own newspapers? And take the bus?" he asked, keeping his voice down.

"Obviously," Ivan said, and settled into an empty seat.

"Though some prefer the subway," Sofia said, and took the handhold.

Stephen sat down beside Ivan. Glancing at the troll, he considered the odds he'd ridden a bus with a troll before and just not known. Before his dad gave him the powder of True Seeing at Chef Nana's funeral, he hadn't been able to see supernormals at all. How many must he have passed on the street back in Chicago without a blink? A bunch, he bet.

"Now," Ivan said, as the bus lumbered through the busy streets, "the Cabinet of Wonders is a museum of sorts. It's a repository of significant artifacts and other items that have been taken into the Octagon's collection at various points in history."

The bus made its way down Fifth Avenue as Ivan chattered on, explaining that the Cabinet was hidden "beneath the noses of the normal world" in the New York Public Library.

"Oh!" said Stephen. "The place with the lions!"

Sofia and Ivan gave each other what Stephen had started thinking of as their "he's wrong, but should we tell him or not?" look. He still had a lot to learn about the world of supernormal affairs. But . . .

"I've seen pictures of them," he protested as the bus came to a halt.

Ignoring him, Sofia skipped toward the opening door. "This is our stop!" she said.

In fact, as they got off the bus together, the library looked *exactly* like pictures Stephen had seen of it online. Patrons, tourists, and people who seemed to just be hanging out crowded the sidewalk out front and the stone stairs leading up to a pair of large doors. And there, flanking the stairs on either side, was the pair of world-famous lion statues.

Except they weren't statues.

And they weren't lions.

CHAPTER TWO

The two crouching figures perched on the stone plinths had the *bodies* of lions, but they also had enormous pairs of folded wings, and their heads were those of gigantic humans. The one on the right was gigantic anyway; the one on the left had the features of a girl about Stephen's age, and was much smaller.

"Sphinxes?" Stephen asked. "The lions at the New York Public Library are sphinxes?"

"Obviously," Ivan said.

Sofia laughed as Stephen blinked.

The girl sphinx spotted them. "Ivan! Hullo!" she called out in a chirpy voice. "Here to try your luck again?"

Ivan didn't answer her, instead striding over to address the much larger sphinx, who shared the other's dark complexion but had tangled eyebrows and a bushy beard. "Greetings, Hakor," Ivan said. "I wish to pose a riddle to you."

Sofia whispered to Stephen, "He does this every time."

Hakor's mouth curved in amusement, but the larger sphinx sat up from his crouch and addressed Ivan formally. "Greetings, Ivanos. As I have reminded you before, my petite human friend, this usually works the other way around."

Sofia said, "Ivan thinks if he can stump Hakor with a riddle, it'll prove he's smarter than Bek."

"Who's Bek?" Stephen asked.

The smaller sphinx bounded down from her place and poked her head in between Stephen's and Sofia's. "*I'm* Bek. It's short for Bekhetamun. And I never claimed to be smarter than Ivan, but it's not like I'm just going to let him win at trivia now, is it? That wouldn't be fair."

"Sphinxes are big believers in fair play," said Sofia. "Right, Bek?"

"The biggest and the fairest," said Bek, with a nod of her pointy chin.

Someday Stephen would get used to things like *having a conversation with a sphinx*, but today was not that day.

Ivan, meanwhile, had drawn forth a leather-bound notebook from inside his jacket pocket. He paged through it quickly, and Stephen was surprised to see that Ivan looked nervous. Ivan was usually supremely confident . . . except perhaps around any supernormal night creatures.

"Ah," said Ivan, pausing on a page, then shaking his head and continuing. He cleared his throat. "If you'll just give me a moment more to find it. A riddle of my own devising."

A young woman tapped Stephen on the shoulder. "Pardon me," she said in a British accent. "Would you mind taking a picture of us in front of the lion?" She gestured toward the empty spot where Bek had been sitting a moment before.

Stephen looked around and realized that nobody had reacted to the young sphinx leaping down onto the sidewalk.

"The library maintains the illusion of the statues

even when we aren't at our stations," Bek explained helpfully. "Though we're always close by."

The British woman was still holding her phone out to Stephen, smiling, so he said, "Sure thing," and took it from her. Another young woman joined the first, and they hammed it up in front of the empty plinth. As he snapped the picture, Stephen saw the image of a stone lion behind the pair on the screen. He handed the phone back with a smile.

"Here we go," said Sofia, and tugged on his arm.

Ivan had found the page he was looking for. He squinted at the notebook and spoke:

"I grind down mountains,
cover all in my way.
My only fear is
a sunny day."

Ivan raised his head. "Well?" he said.

The amused look had not left Hakor's broad, wrinkled face. "A fine effort, my young friend Ivanos, but you have not stumped me today. I shall let my apprentice answer this one, I think."

Bek sounded a delighted purr deep in her throat. She strode over to Ivan. When she sat on her haunches, the tips of her folded wings were higher than Ivan's head.

Stephen moved in close and pushed the notebook against Ivan's chest to prevent peeking.

Bek sniffed. "As if I would ever cheat. Or need to!" She paused and then winked. "Ivan, the answer to your riddle is . . . a glacier!"

"Well done, Bekhetamun," Hakor said. Bek grinned and made that purring sound again.

Ivan didn't say anything, and Stephen worried he was taking the riddle answering hard. "Hey, yeah! That makes sense. Good one, Ivan!" he said.

"Not good enough," said Ivan. He frowned and stowed his notebook.

"Cheer up, Ivan," said Sofia. "Sphinxes are the riddle masters of the supernormal world. If you could stump Hakor and Bek, they wouldn't be very good at their jobs, would they?"

"A fair point," Ivan said.

Hakor appeared to be biting back a laugh. But when he spoke, he said, "If anyone could stump us, it would be you, Ivanos."

Ivan relaxed, giving Hakor a more confident nod.

Stephen was still curious, though. "What *are* your jobs?" he asked.

"We serve as guardians of the Cabinet of Wonders," said Hakor.

Stephen nodded. "So, nobody can go in without answering a riddle, right?"

"Not exactly," said Bek. "The Cabinet is open for visitation by most members of the supernormal community. We prevent the removal of the magical items stored there."

"Oh," said Stephen. "The riddles don't really figure into it at all?"

"Riddles figure into *everything* to do with sphinxes," said Ivan.

Hakor nodded gravely. "They are, in fact, bound up in our very natures. If someone were to successfully answer a riddle posed by myself or my apprentice, then they would have the freedom to choose any item in the Cabinet for their own use."

That didn't sound like a particularly good security system to Stephen, and Bek must have guessed the line of his thoughts. "Nobody's correctly answered a sphinx's riddle in more than four thousand years," she said. "Anyway, you still haven't introduced yourself! Though I'm pretty sure I know who you are. You're Cindermass's friend, right? The boy who saved the day at his birthday party?"

Stephen blushed, and before he could think of anything to say, Hakor spoke. "Which makes you the son of Princess Aria of the Primrose Court, recently returned from exile. It is an honor to meet you, young sir. Any friend of Ivan's."

Ivan puffed up under Hakor's regard.

"And Sofia's!" Bek added. Sofia tipped an imaginary hat to her.

"Thank you," Stephen said. "My name's Stephen Lawson. My dad just took over as chef at the New Harmonia."

"Of course," Hakor said. "Please extend our warmest regards to both of your parents."

"I heard you all almost got made into servants of that brat Lady Sarabel of the Court of Thorns for a hundred years or something," said Bek. "Is that true? And that your dad almost lost his job because he served a vampire a garlic omelet? And that you outsmarted everyone?"

"That's . . . not *exactly* what happened," Stephen said. He was blushing again. The sphinxes had heard this much about him and his family?

"Bekhetamun," Hakor said. "Please remember to conduct yourself with some degree of decorum."

The young sphinx crossed her eyes and stuck her tongue out, then leaped back up to her spot on the stone pediment. "Let all who come before me know the gravity of my task!" she said, deepening her voice and sounding more than a little bit like Hakor. "Should you seek to retrieve an item from the vaults below this place of learning, you must answer my riddle!"

Sofia cracked up, and Ivan shook his head, grinning. Only Stephen noticed that a man sitting at a small metal table nearby turned and gazed at Bek as she joked around. How had he not noticed the guy before? He was practically sitting on top of them—and the way he was dressed!

The man was completely bizarre, from head to toe. He had long black hair held back in a braid, which peeked out below his flamboyant hat. The feathered hat looked like something from the cover of a Three Musketeers book. He also sported a heavy red-and-black cloak woven with ringed planets, sparkly tailed comets, and mathematical symbols.

"You should be careful about saying such things, little one," the man said, maintaining his intent gaze as he stood up and stalked over to stand in front of Bek. He had a strange tattoo on one side of his face, the dark swirling ink disappearing down his throat into the collar of a yellow silk shirt. "Someone might take you up on it."

Bek's eyes widened. "You can see me?"

"Of course." The man shrugged. "I am a powerful sorcerer. I was just waiting for your visitors to be on their way. But I'm not particularly known for my patience."

Stephen shot a look at his friends. Ivan had his eyes narrowed, the way he did when he was trying to figure something out. Sofia's hands formed loose fists, like she was getting ready for a fight. The man was a *sorcerer*? A *powerful* sorcerer? Stephen knew there was a witch on the Octagon, but he hadn't met her in person yet.

"Um, cool." Stephen attempted to be nice, despite his friends' reactions. "What *are* you known for? Are you here to see the Cabinet of Wonders, too?"

The man lifted one side of his mouth in a mocking half grin. "My name is Edmund. Soon to be the name those who fear and adore me whisper into the darkness: Edmund the Enchanter."

Not the scariest name Stephen had ever heard.

When they didn't react, the man continued. "I'm Edmund *Darkfell*. And if there were any justice, *you* would know that *my* knowledge of all things mystical, magical, and even mathematical is as unparalleled as my skill with sorcery, spells, and all things supernormal."

"*Oh.*" Ivan sounded impressed. "The Darkfells

are some of the most powerful magic users in the Western Hemisphere," he said to Stephen. But then he squinted back at the man. "I've never heard of an Edmund, though."

"That is about to change, my dapper young friend," Edmund said, almost spitting the words. This guy clearly had some issues. "As for what I want"—and he turned to Hakor—"I invoke my right of challenge, as any who come before you may. Hakor of the Nile, I demand a riddle. Your apprentice just offered to pose one. Would you rather it come from her?"

Something scary flashed in Hakor's amber eyes. "As you clearly know, the challenge for a riddle cannot be denied," he boomed. "However, Bekhetamun *is* still my apprentice, and that means her riddle is not yet set. It will be me."

"As I thought," Edmund said, with a wink. "So, ask me."

"Hold on!" Bek whipped a small hourglass with wood and brass embellishments out of nowhere and held it high. "You will have the five minutes to

respond. You may request a riddle only once. All within the sound of my voice will be magically prevented from telling anyone Hakor's riddle after they leave this place—including you—should you not be able to answer correctly." She gave the enchanter a smug smile. "Good luck. You'll need it."

Edmund nodded to Hakor. "Go on. Ask."

Hakor's deep voice rung out:

"It arcs high,
twixt those that fly,
if it strikes true,
then you die."

Hakor moved not a muscle when he finished, but gave off an air of confidence nonetheless. Bek turned the hourglass, and sand began to fall.

"Hard one," Ivan said, stroking his chin.

"I wouldn't even try it," Sofia agreed.

"Me neither," Stephen said. He couldn't imagine what the answer could be.

Bek bounced up and down, watching the sand, clearly expecting Edmund to fail, too.

Edmund swept off his hat and struck a pose, pointing one finger in the air. He paced back and forth in front of Hakor. "So much depends on those fourteen words. Let us examine them, each in turn."

"Does he think he's teaching a *class*?" asked Sofia.

"'It'!" Edmund explained. "'It' is a pronoun, and pronouns must have antecedents that must be nouns. Nouns are persons, places, things, or ideas, and in this case, the noun is the solution to the riddle."

Stephen rolled his eyes. "If he goes through all fourteen words this way, he's going to bust his time limit."

The sand streamed through Bek's hourglass.

Edmund pontificated on. "'Arcs,' in this case, is a verb—our mysterious 'it' is moving along a curving path."

Ivan whispered, "He's talking this out the same way I would. You don't suppose . . ."

Edmund snapped his fingers, apparently to get their attention. "'Twixt those that fly'—old-fashioned word, *twixt*, but then you *are* thousands of years old, aren't you Hakor? Never mind, don't answer—I'm aware that would break the rules of offering your riddle. 'If it strikes,' and there's our 'it' again and another clue, because now we know 'it' is something that can strike, and more, we know from the last line that when 'it' strikes, 'you'—and I suppose that's meant to be *me*—'die.'

"But I will not die from any arcing strike, just as I will not fail to answer this riddle." Edmund the Enchanter grinned. "The answer is simple."

They all waited. Stephen held his breath.

Sofia said, "Come on. Don't stop talking *now*! What's your guess?"

"I don't have a guess; I have the answer." Edmund eyed Bek's hourglass, and said, "Only one thing arcs between 'those that fly'—in this case, between a specific creature's wings—to strike dead what stands before it.

"A wyvern's sting."

Hakor blinked.

"Is that right?" Stephen asked, glancing from Ivan to Bek, both of whom seemed to be stunned into silence, and then to Sofia, who shrugged, her face pinched. She looked as worried as Stephen felt.

"Is that the right answer?" he asked again, this time speaking to Hakor, who remained perfectly still.

"Of course it is," said Edmund the Enchanter. "And now if you'll give me the pass? Places to go, a prize to claim." This last was directed at Hakor.

Hakor hesitated, oh so briefly, then raised one terrifyingly sharp claw in response. Stephen feared the sphinx was about to cut the enchanter down, which he could sympathize with—the guy seemed like a pompous jerk. But Hakor simply tapped the man on the shoulder.

"You . . . may pass, Enchanter. The Docent, as well as the Unseen Guardians, will allow you to retrieve a single item of your choice from the Cabinet below."

"Wait!" Ivan said. "He can't just take anything! Some of the most powerful items in the supernormal world are stored in the Cabinet. Some of the deadliest!"

"A riddle has been asked and answered," said the enchanter. "Now I'll take what's mine by right and look good doing it. Please tell everyone you see." He whirled, his long cloak flowing like a bedazzled cloud behind him as he marched up the steps.

Stephen thought fast. "We should go after him," he said. "See what he takes!"

Hakor said, "Yes, you must. The Docent is bound to the library, and the Unseen Guardians do not speak. Someone must report to the Octagon what has happened here, and they will need to know what this warlock has taken. I fear the worst."

"I fear that has already happened," Bek said, gazing at Hakor, no lightness left in her voice.

"Hush now," Hakor said softly. "Go," he prompted them. "Be quick."

Stephen, Ivan, and Sofia raced up the stairs, following Edmund the Enchanter.

CHAPTER THREE

Stephen would have liked to stop and look around at the inside of the library—its grandeur was almost a match for the New Harmonia. But there was no time for that. He, Ivan, and Sofia flew through the security checkpoint, shoes thudding on the marble. The guards didn't even seem to see them— or Edmund the Enchanter, whose black cloak was flying behind him as he disappeared through a golden door.

"We'd better hurry," Ivan said.

They reached the golden door, and Stephen blinked at the ornate sign beside it.

ENTER THE CABINET OF WONDERS. BE ASTONISHED AT THIS COLLECTION,

**PRIZED BEYOND ALL OTHERS.
OBEY THE DOCENT.
DO NOT TROUBLE THE UNSEEN
GUARDIANS WITHOUT CAUSE.
ENTER AT YOUR OWN PERIL.**

"This sounds dangerous," Stephen said.

"It's not our immediate peril I'm worried about." Ivan reached to push open the door.

Or wait—maybe Ivan wasn't pushing the door, after all. He let his hand linger on its surface, and Sofia pressed hers there beside his. She had tiny sword decals on her fingernails.

"Stephen, you, too," she said. "It has to record our entrance and agree to let us in."

"Oh." Stephen stood beside Ivan and spread his fingers wide on the cool, shiny surface.

After a moment, the door sighed open. Stephen, Ivan, and Sofia stepped inside the Cabinet of Wonders.

Spotlit cases and pedestals lined the long

entryway. On one side, Stephen saw a diamond skull on a red pillow. A small note underneath called it the "Skull of Diamonda, High Princess of Pluto, and later, Empress of Atlantis." Opposite sat a massive hammer in a case, labeled "Asgardian Hammer."

Wait. Was that *Thor's?*

It was difficult not to stop and look at everything and start asking a million questions, because, *Thor's hammer* and a *space empress ruling Atlantis.* But Stephen had to keep moving so as not to get left behind by Ivan and Sofia. They finally emerged from the treasure-lined hallway into an immense museumlike room. Shelves with large old books, several of which lay open, lined one wall. And dotting the rest of the space were more cases, pedestals, and pillow stands like those on the way in, all lit to show off their treasures.

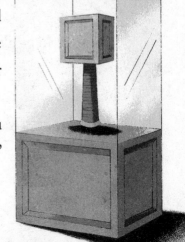

"I suppose this is where you tell me not to touch anything,"

said Stephen. His fingers itched not just to touch, but to whip out his sketchbook to try to capture the weird bounty that surrounded them.

"You can try," said Sofia. "The Unseen Guardians would stop you, though."

Stephen scanned the room, but being named the Unseen Guardians probably meant he wouldn't be able to see them. "Stop me gently, I hope," he said.

"The first time, at least," replied Ivan.

They passed a slowly rotating display of a sword stuck through a manhole lid. Writing was carved into the thick metal edge of the lid, and Stephen paused to read it: WHOSOEVER SHALL DRAW FORTH THIS SWORD FROM THIS MANHOLE LID SHALL REIGN AS MONARCH OF ALL NEW YORK CITY.

Sofia waved her hand in front of Stephen's face. "Come on."

Stephen kept glancing from side to side as they made their way briskly into the depths of the Cabinet. Some things, like the painting of the lady with the mysterious smile, he sort of recognized. Though he didn't think she'd had horns in the reproductions he'd seen. Other objects, like the clockwork canary tunelessly whistling inside a copper wire cage, were inexplicable. But most of the treasures on display were simply baffling. Why would a Cabinet dedicated to preserving powerful and dangerous items display a pair of bowling shoes under lock and key? What could possibly be powerful *or* dangerous about a box of crayons that were all the same shade of green?

"There he is!" Stephen said, spotting Edmund the Enchanter's floppy, feathered hat near the center of the room.

"The Docent doesn't look so hot," Sofia said as they made their way closer.

Stephen didn't know how Sofia could tell. The Docent stood in front of Edmund. Well, hovered there, because the Docent didn't appear to have feet. Where legs might have been was a wispy vapor that grew more solid the farther up you looked. The Docent's chest was much larger than the wisps below, and its deeply lined face was pale shades of green and purple and blue.

"Is the Docent a genie?" Stephen asked.

"Sort of," Sofia said.

"More or less," Ivan agreed.

They went silent, finally close enough to hear the exchange taking place.

"You have answered Hakor's riddle," the Docent said. "And you say you're a Darkfell?"

"You know that I did," Edmund said. "And yes, I am. Now let me take what I came for."

"I don't suppose there's any way I can stop you." The Docent fluttered, fading and then solidifying again.

"Not without breaking the law," Edmund said. "Something a Docent such as yourself would *never* dream of."

"Only because they're *good*," Sofia murmured, sounding angry.

"Careful, child," the Docent said, turning to look right at them. "Do not interfere. Let this . . . danger . . . leave us."

"After I receive my reward," Edmund said. "But I'm glad you realize that I'm dangerous. Soon everyone will—but something tells me they won't mind once they've learned it." And then he laughed.

Stephen didn't know whether to snort or tremble. Did truly dangerous people go around bragging about it? He didn't think so. But then again, Ivan *had* said the Darkfells were masters of magic, and this guy had successfully answered a sphinx's riddle.

Edmund glowered at the Docent. "Now stop delaying."

"Fine," the Docent said. "Reveal the item you desire, and it shall be yours."

There was a gust, as if of wind, and the Docent's long purple hair whipped with it. Edmund's cloak flew up over his head.

"The Unseen Guardians," Ivan said, low.

Edmund threw his cloak back over his shoulders. "The ivory wand of Dadelion."

The Docent gasped, but its exclamation was almost swallowed by another gust of that strange wind. Stephen's hair ruffled as it passed by them, and in moments, a spindly white wand wafted through the air to the Docent. The wand was nearly paper-white and curved into a long, thin crescent moon shape.

"This item is ancient and powerful indeed," said the Docent. "You know what it can do?"

"I know everything about it," Edmund said. "Almost as if its maker were an old friend."

"Are all magic users like this?" Stephen muttered.

"Some of them can be quite vain," Sofia said.

"I still can't believe he answered the riddle," Ivan whispered, almost to himself. "And so easily."

Edmund held out his hand, and though the Docent hesitated, it placed the wand carefully onto his palm. "I beg that you would not use this for ill," the Docent said.

"I am soon to be the most legendary mage of all time," he said. "I will use it for its ultimate purpose."

Edmund the Enchanter closed his fingers around the center of the wand. He lifted it over his head and said a handful of words in a language Stephen didn't recognize. Sparking smoke filled the air around him. Then he turned on his heel to leave.

Stephen started to follow, but Edmund shot a poisonous look over his shoulder. The smile on his face was anything but welcoming. "Stay, young human, stay," Edmund said. "The adults have work to do."

Stephen discovered he didn't have much of a choice. His feet might as well have been glued down. "I can't move," he said, hearing the panic in his voice. He struggled to lift his feet, but they were planted like trees growing into the floor.

As soon as Edmund was out of earshot, Sofia threw her shoulder into Stephen's—*hard*.

"Hey! That hurt!" he said, rubbing his shoulder. He tried again to move his feet, but nothing happened.

"Sorry," Sofia said. "And not sorry. I thought that would work."

"The Cabinet of Wonders is my domain." The Docent floated to Stephen and placed spectral fingers atop his shoulders. "At least for the time being. I have the power to release you, and so I do."

To Stephen's relief, as soon as the Docent's

wispy hand pulled back, he was able to step off the spot. "Thank you."

Ivan's brow was furrowed. "Hakor told us to find out what Edmund was after, and now we have."

"But what does Wordy the Wizard there plan to do with the wand?" Sofia said.

Stephen looked toward the corridor, barely catching a last whirl of Edmund's cloak as the enchanter left the Cabinet. "I don't know how we'll find out unless we follow him," he said. "He seems like the kind of villain who might announce his evil plan upfront just to brag."

The floating form of the Docent loomed over the three of them. "Did you say that Hakor sent you in here? Then he's all right? But oh no, that means . . . poor little Bek!"

Sofia answered the Docent. "She's fine, too. They were both just worried about what that creep would take after he answered Hakor's riddle. We're supposed to warn the Octagon. Which probably means our parents, I guess, since it's not like the Octagon will listen to three kids."

Ivan stuck one finger up in the air. "You forget," he said, "one of us has a parent *on* the Octagon."

Smoky rivulets were trailing down over the Docent's sharp-boned cheeks, emanating from the glowing orbs of its eyes.

Stephen tugged at the floating being's robes. It had said that this was its domain *for now*. "Are you crying? Are you going to lose your job because Edmund took one of the items stored here?"

The Docent peered down at him. "No, child of two worlds, I am in no immediate danger, though it is kind of you to ask after me. It is just that I knew Hakor of the Nile even before we both came into service here at the Cabinet. I knew him for many, many years."

Why was the Docent talking about Hakor in the past tense? But a sudden tap-tap-tapping noise distracted Stephen. "Let's go!" Sofia called, tugging on his arm.

Because the sounds were Ivan's hard-soled shoes smacking against the marble floor as he ran for the exit. Raced for the exit, in fact. Stephen had never seen Ivan move so quickly.

"We'll figure out what's going on and get that wand back!" Stephen blurted, and then took off running after Sofia, who'd almost caught up to Ivan. "Don't worry!"

The three burst, one after another, from the Cabinet door and tore through the crowds in the library's main hallway. Ivan never slowed down, somehow finding a path through the teeming tourists and library patrons to the street doors. Stephen finally caught up with the other two next to Hakor's pediment. Ivan, stricken, lifted a hand in midair and then lowered it, as though he didn't know what to do.

Unlike the Docent's, Bek's tears could never be mistaken for anything else. She had her head thrown back, howling wordlessly at the sky as she cried and pawed helplessly at Hakor.

Hakor, who had turned to solid stone.

CHAPTER FOUR

Ivan sat beside a closed pair of richly carved wooden doors while Sofia and Stephen paced in front of him. The Octagon was in session within, and they were waiting to be called upon to give their report.

After they'd discovered Hakor, everything became a blur. Sofia had called the hotel, and her mother had sent her father and a handful of guards to see to them and Bek. Julio had bundled them into a car and brought them here. The guards had agreed to stay with Bek until she calmed down—which might be never. Julio had gone in to announce their presence to the Octagon's attendants and then been dismissed, leaving them in this waiting chamber with its impossibly high, vaulted ceiling and intricately tiled floor.

Stephen stared down at his sneakers and admired the level of detail in the Octagon symbol he was walking across. The dark cave mouth representing subterranean dwellers showed stalactites and stalagmites like the fangs of some fierce creature.

"Did either of you notice anything odd about Edmund's behavior?" Ivan asked.

Stephen and Sofia both stopped pacing.

"He's an odd dude," Stephen said. "But I'm guessing that's not what you mean."

"It's not," Ivan said, stroking his chin. He was thinking.

"What did you notice, Ivan?" Sofia asked.

"I'm not sure yet," Ivan said distractedly.

Stephen followed Sofia to the other end of the room when she began to pace again. "Is Ivan going to be okay? I could tell Hakor was special to him."

Sofia pitched her voice so that only Stephen would hear her. "Hakor was Ivan's hero. He's looked up to him forever."

Stephen wanted to say something to Ivan that would comfort him or cheer him up. But he had no

idea what it might be. Or even if it was a good idea
to try. When Stephen and his father had moved here
to New York after his grandmother died, nothing
anybody had said had made him feel better about
that, really. He still missed Chef Nana every day.
But on the other hand . . . he did like talking about
her, remembering things they'd done together or
hearing stories about her from his dad.

Stephen walked over to Ivan. "Hey, Ivan, how
did you get to know Hakor?"

Ivan startled. "What?"

"I guess your parents probably took you to the
library a lot when you were little, right?" Stephen
asked. "Is that how you met Hakor?"

"I don't remember ever *not* going to the library,"
he said. "I don't remember ever not knowing Hakor.
I remember when Bek came here, though. Hakor's
old apprentice got the job guarding the Vault of
Mists in Kyoto. That was just a few years ago."

There must be a lot more sphinxes than Stephen
had ever guessed. "Sphinxes in Japan, too?" he said.
"I only ever saw pictures of the one in Egypt."

"The Great Sphinx, Khafre," said Sofia. She came over and sat down beside Ivan, squeezing his shoulder. "That's the one most humans have heard of, yes."

"The one most humans think is just a statue," Ivan added. "But until the dragon Kindlefleur answered Khafre's riddle four thousand years ago and turned him to stone, what we now call the Great Sphinx was considered among the wisest and most powerful supernormals. He was a ruler in the ancient world. I can't believe I forgot about how he came to be what he is now."

"So that's just what happens to them?" Stephen asked. "To sphinxes, I mean? If somebody can answer their riddles—"

"Then they turn to stone, yes," said Ivan. "It's only happened once in all of recorded history. Well, twice."

"Twice counting Hakor?" Stephen asked. That seemed impossible.

"Yes," said Ivan. "The riddles of the sphinxes are not *supposed* to be solved. That's why they each only have one. When Kindlefleur answered the Great

Sphinx and took the treasure he guarded into her hoard, she was cast out of supernormal society. It's widely suspected that she'd stolen the answer from the sacred Grove of Memory in the sphinxes' city, the Hall of Sand and Wind. Though no one was ever able to prove it. At that time, the Hall of Sand and Wind was open to all. Since that day, they've admitted no outsiders. Even Kindlefleur's own clutchmates never spoke to her again."

Their friend Cindermass the dragon, back at the New Harmonia, certainly abided by a lot of rules. Stephen had managed to use the draconic code to his advantage, but it hadn't been easy. He imagined that dragons could give an extreme roasting when they wanted to.

The doors next to Ivan and Sofia swung open.

But there was nobody there.

"Down here!" came a squeaking voice.

On the floor, a gray mouse wearing an ornate, if tiny, uniform and an indignant expression stared up at them. "I am Sigmund Dormouse, Watcher of the Ways."

 The mouse seemed to be expecting some kind of response. Luckily Sofia was on it. She might not want to be a diplomat like her mother when she grew up—instead she wanted to follow in her dad's footsteps as captain of the guard—but she still knew almost all the rules and had a good touch with diplomacy, too.

"Of course!" she said. "Your fame as the gatekeeper of the Octagon precedes you, Sigmund. I am Sofia Gutierrez, a human girl, and these are Ivanos La Doyt, a human boy, and Stephen Lawson, half fae."

"And half human," Stephen added. "What kind of mouse are you?"

"He's a *rodentia magicae*," Ivan said, then, pausing. "A magical rodent."

"I can speak for myself! And I know who you all are, of course," the mouse grumbled. "You weren't on the schedule for today, but apparently *some* people believe who they're *related* to means they can ignore *protocol*."

The mouse glared at Stephen.

"Me?" he asked. "I didn't know we were breaking any protocols. I thought Julio talked to you? Sofia's dad? The Knight Martial? We didn't just show up. I didn't say anything to my mom, if that's what you mean."

"Hmmph," the mouse replied. "When even the representatives ignore the rules and regulations regarding scheduling, it's a sign of how bad things have gotten. Yes, it surely is." The mouse had been standing up on his hind legs while he spoke, but now he turned, dropped to all fours, and started to skitter into the darkness beyond the door.

"Are we supposed to follow him?" Stephen asked. Before Ivan or Sofia could answer, Sigmund Dormouse did.

"Yes!" shouted the mouse. "And don't look down!"

The mouse's warning made sense only once the door had closed behind them, and they discovered that they were on a narrow walkway suspended in midair. Dark gray mists billowed all around, above and below. Stephen couldn't see any source for the dim light.

"Have you considered handrails?" Sofia asked, grabbing hold of Ivan's belt to steady him in front of her.

But Sigmund was either too far ahead of them to hear or ignoring them. He bounded along the walkway at a very high rate of speed, even for a mouse, and the three of them had to hurry along, trusting their balance.

After a few minutes, they came to a spiral staircase extending upward into the mist. Sigmund waited for them at its first step.

"Up you go," he said. "The Octagon awaits in the Floorless Chamber. It's customary at this point for me to offer a word of advice on how to avoid falling into the Bottomless Fog, but obviously nobody cares about customs anymore." With a last huff, he darted back the way they had come, disappearing from sight.

"That's kind of a rude magical mouse," said Stephen.

Sofia nodded in agreement. But Ivan started

climbing the stairs, pausing just long enough to draw a round brass instrument from one of his many interior pockets. Stephen thought it was a watch at first, but when Ivan opened its lid, he saw that it was some kind of compass. The needle was spinning around and around, never coming to rest on any of the numerous letters and symbols etched around its circumference.

"Just as I suspected," said Ivan. "I've always heard that the Floorless Chamber exists in a protected locale. Now I can state without doubt that we are in the Folds."

Stephen tried to remember if he'd seen an entry for the Folds in *An Almanack of the Mores and Ways of Supernormal Kind*, but came up with nothing. He was about to ask what Ivan was talking about, but Sofia surprised him by speaking up first.

"The Folds?" she asked. "What's that mean? I've never heard of anything called the Folds."

Usually Stephen was the one who hadn't heard of anything Sofia or Ivan had to say about supernormal things.

Ivan cleared his throat, hemming and hawing as they started up the stairs. "The Folds are the spaces between spaces. When beings travel from our world to Faery, for example, they journey through the Folds, even though they don't realize it. The gateways at the New Harmonia are native to the Folds."

"And you know this how?" Sofia asked.

"Erm, well, this is all discussed in the *Forbidden Journals of Marie Curie*. Which of course you haven't read."

Sofia stopped climbing and folded her arms. "I haven't read the *Forbidden Journals*, Ivan, because they're *forbidden*. Where did you even find a copy? I know there's not one in the hotel's library, and even our special library cards wouldn't let us check it out if there was. That book is only available to the Octagon and its knights on a need-to-know basis."

This was getting more interesting by the second, and Stephen wondered how he could get one of those special library cards. Ivan's cheeks were growing red, though. Maybe Sofia needed a reminder that

Ivan was coping as best he could. Fighting about secret books could wait.

"I'm sure Ivan has a perfectly reasonable explanation about why he did something forbidden." Stephen himself would never be famous for following rules and was kind of relieved to hear that Ivan might have broken a pretty big one.

"Perfectly reasonable, right," said Sofia. "Ivan? Do your parents know you've been nosing around in their belongings again?"

Ivan almost missed a stair, but righted himself before he fell.

"I'll be allowed to read the journals when I become an official m-master of detection and mystical m-mysteries anyway," he stammered, and seemed about to say more when a clanking noise from below interrupted.

Stephen looked down.

He could no longer see the walkway or the bottom steps. *Have we climbed that far already?* But no. As he watched, a step disappeared with a clank, and then another. "Um, guys, maybe we'd better figure this out later, because the staircase is disappearing from under us! Climb!"

"Probably Sigmund Rude-Mouse thinks we're taking too long," Sofia said.

They rushed ahead, Sofia grabbing Ivan's arm so she could tow him up faster. The clanks continued to follow them until at last, they reached the top of the stairs and leaped onto a flat surface at the top.

"That was close," Stephen said, sucking in a deep breath as he peered back the way they'd come.

The last stair vanished into the platform they stood on. A platform in the shape of an Octagon, surrounded by empty air on all sides. Sofia had reached out to take his arm, too, holding tight so none of them fell.

"We're here," Ivan said, pressing his glasses up on his nose. "Greetings, most high and exalted members of the Octagon."

CHAPTER FIVE

Stephen looked up and blinked to find a fuzzy-faced mole man wearing small round glasses sitting directly in front of them, on the other side of a narrow moat of air. The platform they stood on was ringed by a much bigger octagon-shaped table with an . . . individual . . . seated at each flat side.

The Floorless Chamber, the mouse had said. The Bottomless Fog still swirled around and below them. *Great.*

They'd better not make any sudden movements.

In addition to the mole man, who must represent the subterranean dwellers, Stephen could see Trevor the bigfoot's mother, Roams over Rivers and Mountains, who nodded at them, and a mermaid so beautiful even looking at her made Stephen blush.

Of course, Stephen had learned at the hotel that seeing *any* mermaid would make him blush—mermaids enchanted all who looked upon them unless they actively decided not to.

The mermaid wore a dress of shells that showed off pinkish scales on her arms and legs. She now stood behind a fishbowl placed directly on the table. Inside the bowl, the eyes of a small, bright yellow-and-white-striped fish peered round and black through the glass.

Huh, Stephen thought. *I wouldn't have imagined the sea people would be represented by a mermaid with a pet fish.*

Bubbles floated through the water around the mouth of the fish, and the mermaid said, "They aren't. They are represented by the Kraken, who attends by proxy, although she sleeps. You would not want her to fully wake. She is telepathically linked to Sir Aqueous Fin of the Reefs, who can read minds if he chooses."

Stephen felt a pinch from Sofia, as though he needed to be told he'd screwed up. "I'm, um, so sorry," he said. Even he knew that a Kraken was a giant sea monster. And that waking one up would be extremely bad. "I didn't mean to think out loud. At all. You know what I mean. I didn't mean to think at all. . . ."

The mermaid's lips quirked in faint amusement. Stephen blushed harder and shut up.

"Welcome," the mole man said in a deep voice, giving Stephen an excuse to focus on him instead. "I am Magister Otis, the current chair of the Octagon. Thank you for coming. We have the bare details of what happened—that a riddle was answered and an item removed. We are grateful you can offer a first-hand account of precisely what has occurred."

"I'm so sorry you witnessed such an event. How are you?" a new voice asked.

The platform spun slowly around to face the speaker, but Stephen already knew who it was: his mother.

She wore a tiara with jewels in the shape of flowers, and a fancy dress that complemented her pale blue skin. On her left was Count von Morgenstierne—a vampire Stephen definitely was not fond of—who bared his fangs at the three of them. A grimace, a smile; it could be tough to know with this particular vampire. On his mother's right sat a woman with long, luxurious red hair topped by a pointy hat. A black cat lay curled in her lap, and its face was barely visible. She must be the witch.

"Hi, Mom," Stephen said, swallowing. "We've, uh, had quite a day."

"So I've heard." Her eyes swept up and down him. "You are unharmed? All three of you?"

Stephen glanced at Ivan. "Yes. But Hakor's not. He's turned to stone."

"We know," she said.

"A great tragedy," said another voice, and the platform rotated again. Stephen clutched Sofia's arm to steady himself. "It is a shock that anyone correctly answered Hakor's riddle."

The comments came from a woman with dark skin, wearing half-mooned glasses that slid down her nose so far she couldn't actually be using them to help her vision.

"As you might imagine, the riddle wasn't exactly easy either, Aminata," Ivan said, his frown back, eyebrows pinching together.

"The guy didn't even hesitate, really. He just talked his way through it," Stephen added. "Ami . . ." He trailed off when he realized he hadn't quite gotten her name when Ivan said it.

"May I introduce Aminata Aya," Sofia said. "Human representative of the Octagon, from the city of Timbuktu."

The woman inclined her head to Stephen, her glasses somehow not tipping off her nose. *"Ahwarrenfoke, yungkind."*

What did it mean? "Um, hi," Stephen tried.

His mother spoke behind them. "The boy doesn't know any fae dialects yet."

"Of course not," Aminata said. "At any rate, it is very surprising *anyone* answered any sphinx's riddle. But it seems that it has happened, nonetheless."

A loud squawk sounded beside her, and the platform shifted a fraction in the direction of the winged member beside her. The bird was larger than a normal-size human, with intelligent eyes and beautiful feathers that glowed the red, orange, and yellow of flickering firelight.

"Since a dragon was the last to correctly solve a sphinx's riddle, then perhaps a dragon is involved again," the glowing bird said, voice masculine. "A gossipy one. Anyone know such a being who currently resides in this city?"

Does he mean Cindermass? Stephen wondered.

"Now, now, Chenghiz," Aminata said. "Don't let the firebird folk's history with the dragons color your judgment. That seems incredibly far-fetched."

The bird's fiery feathers ruffled. "I simply know more about them, having grown up with the legends of the battles my ancestors fought on the steppes. They could be cheaters themselves."

"No way Cindermass would hang out with this guy," Stephen said, offended on their friend's behalf. "Or help him cheat."

Sofia muttered something he couldn't make out.

The bird tilted his head at Stephen, and his beak opened.

But the firebird subsided as Aminata raised a small hand, and said, "I didn't mean to imply there was cheating, only that it's surprising. The sphinxes' city is nigh impenetrable now. No outsiders could access the Grove of Memory without the express approval of the sphinxes' leader—which is never granted."

"Cheating," Ivan murmured to himself.

"If I may interrupt," Magister Otis said. "The tragedy that befell Hakor aside, we have more pressing business with these three."

The platform began to turn slowly back in the mole man's direction. . . .

"May I direct the questions?" asked a lilting voice.

"I suppose," Magister Otis said.

And the platform stopped in front of the woman in the pointy hat beside Stephen's mother.

"I am Madame Veronika, head witch of the Great Coven," the woman introduced herself. The cat let out a meow. "And this is Jersey Pete, my familiar."

Jersey Pete looked like a straight-from-the-alley

scrapper. Stephen resolved to stay on the good side of his claws.

"It's good to see you again, Madame V.," Sofia said and ducked into a half curtsy. Ivan gave a bow, but he still seemed distracted.

"Pleased to meet you," Stephen said.

"I wish the circumstances were more pleasant," she said. "We were told the riddle answerer is a Darkfell? What was his name?"

"He said it was Edmund the Enchanter," Ivan said. "I'd never heard of him."

"Edmund." Madame Veronika considered, brows pulling together. "Edmund. Why is that familiar?"

Jersey Pete reached up a paw to get her attention and stared into Madame Veronika's face.

"Oh!" she said. "Yes. Now I remember. We were at school together. He was a talented student, but he attempted an advanced spell before he could quite pull it off. It was supposed to make him popular, but instead, it made him forgettable. Hard to notice. I suppose I should have wondered what happened to him. . . . But then, the spell would make that unlikely, even if it weakened over time."

"We didn't even notice him at first." Stephen *almost* felt bad for Edmund the jerk. That sounded like a pretty terrible way for a spell to backfire.

"No, you wouldn't have." Madame Veronika's lips pursed together.

"Who are the Darkfells?" Stephen's mother asked.

"They're an old, noble magical family." Madame Veronika shrugged. "Respectable. Their patriarch, Eddard Darkfell, managed to obtain the clock-work sundial, which in turn allowed him to amass a vast collection of magic items by traveling through time. He only stopped when a paradox threatened the family."

"This Edmund also claimed that he was extremely dangerous," Stephen said.

Sofia said, "More than once. Edmund's definitely conceited."

Ivan was being very quiet, and Stephen saw he was stroking his chin again.

"What object did Edmund select?" Madame Veronika asked.

Ivan finally spoke up. "It was the ivory wand of Dadelion."

She blanched. "Did he say what he intended to do with it?"

"He held it overhead and chanted something in a language I didn't know," Sofia said. "It could have been a spell."

"Oh no," Madame Veronika said.

"What does the wand *do*?" Stephen's mother asked.

Madame Veronika shut her eyes briefly, then opened them. "It dates from the fourth dynasty in Egypt. The ivory wand of Dadelion was taken into possession by the Octagon two thousand years ago. When used during a specific crescent moon cycle, it can allow the wielder to change the way others view reality. Completely. Any way they choose."

"The effect must be limited in duration?" It was Count von Morgenstierne who spoke, and Stephen heard echoing murmurs behind them from the mermaid and the mole man and the giant firebird.

Stephen thought the count must be truly

concerned to speak to someone with a cat in her lap. The undead hated and feared all felines—that was one of the first and weirdest facts Stephen had learned about supernormaldom.

"Yes," Madame Veronika said. But any sense of relief was taken away by what she said next: "It is limited to the lifetime of the caster."

A grumble of dismay circulated throughout the Floorless Chamber.

"Surely," said the bigfoot Roams, in her deep melodic voice, "the effect is also limited in scope."

"I'm afraid not," Madame Veronika said. "It can affect the whole world, should the holder of the wand choose. We will have only until the next crescent moon to discover his intentions and stop him. If we can."

Jersey Pete gazed up at his owner and placed his paw on her hand in comfort.

"When is that?" asked the mole man. "The next crescent moon. Secretary-at-arms, do you know?"

But Ivan had taken another widget out of his pocket, this one gold like the compass but with moons and suns on its face. He rotated a lever on one side and then said, "If I may?"

"Speak," Stephen's mother said.

"The next crescent moon is three nights from tonight."

"We'll need to summon the La Doyts immediately," Aminata said.

"You have a La Doyt right here," Ivan said. "And I believe I have a key piece of information."

"What is it?" Madame Veronika asked.

"Edmund the Enchanter cheated," Ivan declared.

Stephen blinked. "I thought that was impossible."

"Think about it," Ivan said. "Edmund almost seemed to toy with Hakor, pretending to ask for a riddle from Bek. Then . . . the way he held forth. His little speech seemed rehearsed. He knew the answer already."

"It *is* impossible," Aminata said. "The Hall of Sand and Wind is a fortress."

"Be that as it may," Ivan said.

"Ivan's right," Stephen said. Sofia nodded agreement, and he went on, "Edmund did seem awfully comfortable that he'd get the answer. He never even broke a sweat."

"I'm afraid we must focus on the outcome," Madame Veronika said gently but firmly. "It is our duty to prevent whatever Edmund is planning. Thank you for visiting us."

Turning away from the three friends, the members of the Octagon began to buzz about plans and assignments. Veronika would talk with one of the Darkfells to see if they knew anything. Research would be done on what might counteract the effects of the wand.

The trio just stood there. After a few moments, Ivan said to Sofia, "Can you get their attention?"

With a nod, she placed her fingers in her mouth and whistled loudly, as though she was calling a taxi. The room quieted.

"Yes?" Stephen's mother said.

"Aren't you going to do anything to help Hakor?" Ivan asked. "And Bek? Edmund cheated. He gained the wand through ill means. It should be forfeit."

"Sweet child." Madame Veronika clucked with

sympathy. "It is a great tragedy to lose a sphinx. But . . . it is the way of their kind. A new mentor will be sent for Bekhetamun soon. You three have been helpful. You are free to go."

Stephen didn't want to go, and he knew Ivan didn't either. He wanted to argue. How could it be the natural way if it had only happened *twice?* He turned back to his mom, hoping she'd be an ally. But she gave him a nod and then said, "I will see you for painting and dinner tomorrow night. Take care."

The mole man said, "Farewell, young scions," as the platform rotated back to face him, and the spiral stairs began to unfold again, one after another. *Clank, clank, clank.*

They had been dismissed.

CHAPTER
SIX

They didn't talk much on the drive back to the hotel; just rode in quiet frustration. Julio had been waiting to take them home in the New Harmonia's long, low car.

Now he pulled up at the curb in front of the hotel to let them out. Before they exited the car, he said, "Hang on a sec."

Stephen spotted the reason for the delay. The centaur they had seen earlier was leaving the hotel in a distinguished suit, smiling and holding hands with a long-haired gremlin wearing bright red lipstick.

They disappeared up the street, and Julio waved his hand. "The coast is clear. Go on in and get something to eat and some rest."

"I completely forgot about this morning," Stephen said. The ink-splashed centaur was the whole reason they'd been at the library and ended up as witnesses to the disaster. Well, the centaur and playing croquet with the monkeys.

Julio nodded. "You guys have had a long day. Tomorrow will be better."

For them, maybe. But not for Bek. Or Hakor.

Although, Stephen guessed Hakor didn't *feel* anything anymore. If he was going to be replaced, did that mean they'd put his stone remains somewhere else?

It was distressing to think about. And the Octagon seemed to believe they should just let it go. Stephen sometimes thought he'd never understand the rules of this world, and this was one of those times.

"Thanks for the ride, Dad." Sofia climbed out first, then Ivan, then Stephen.

Stephen ducked his head back in to ask Julio a question. "Will the Octagon be able to get the wand back? Stop whatever Edmund plans to do?"

"Don't you worry," Julio said, and shifted the car into drive.

Stephen shut the door, and Julio pulled away. So, the Octagon was completely focused on Edmund the Enchanter. That made sense; given what the wand could apparently do and no indication of Edmund's goal, they had to try to stop him. But where did that leave Hakor? At least now that Stephen, Ivan, and Sofia were back home, they could make their own plans to do . . . something. Right?

When Stephen entered the lobby, his friends were talking to his own dad. Stephen's dad wore his chef's jacket and cap, and he had several white takeaway boxes balanced on one arm easily, with the grace of someone long used to rushing stacks of plates and pans around a kitchen.

"There you are." His dad gave Stephen what was obviously intended to be a comforting smile. "I made some deep-dish pizzas. One for each of you."

Ivan and Sofia plucked their suppers away, and Stephen took the last box. His dad leaned in. "If you need to talk, just wait up. I'll be done in an hour and a half or so."

Stephen nodded. Still, he expected his dad would just tell him to let the Octagon handle everything—even though they planned to do nothing to help Hakor.

Stephen's dad left via the stairwell that went down to the basement kitchens. They'd still be running dinner service at the hotel's restaurant, Ambrosia, even though it was getting late.

The three friends headed across the lobby, passing several of the hotel's magical gateways that some supernormals used to travel over long distances. Stephen was getting a little better at guessing where they went to—the thicket filled with standing stones and people with swords and long tunics and a unicorn must be Avalon. But he had no idea what the next place, filled with a raucous jungle scene, was.

"Where's that?" he asked.

Sofia paused. Then she pointed to where a gleaming golden wall could just be made out behind the thick vegetation. "The Lost City of Z."

He'd never heard of it before, but then it *was* lost. He waited for Ivan to chime in with some facts about it, before realizing Ivan had already reached the elevator and pushed the CALL button. They hurried to catch up with him.

Sofia cracked open her take-out box and sniffed as they waited. "Yum," she said, in a clear attempt to lighten the mood. "I've never had deep-dish before."

"Dad's is—was—the best in Chicago," Stephen said, not quite sure what to make of having a *pizza conversation* after everything that had happened that day.

"I prefer New York style, of course," Ivan said vaguely, staring straight ahead, "but I'll try this pizza cake."

Stephen started to protest that it wasn't cake—at the most a pie—but he stayed quiet until the elevator doors slid open.

"Get on board," the elevator said. "I heard all about your terrible day! What a trial for you! And from the sound of things, we may all be doomed! Who knows what this Edmund the Enchanter plans? Of course, it wouldn't matter for me. What could I do to help prevent the worst? No, I'll just be one of the first affected, whatever happens, powerless to do anything. I just *feel* it. I'm beside myself."

"Edmund's bad news, but the Octagon is on it," Stephen said. Then: "We're going to do something to help Hakor, aren't we?"

Ivan hesitated. "Of course we will do what we can. But more research is required. I'm not entirely certain there is a way to turn a sphinx back from stone."

"Oh," Sofia said, sad. "Right. Look at Khafre."

"Correct," Ivan said.

"But we'll try, won't we?" Stephen asked.

Ivan gave a short nod. "Hakor was my friend."

"I take it Hakor was the sphinx whose riddle this foul Edmund solved?" the elevator said. "What was your friend like?"

Sofia opened her mouth to speak, but Ivan answered, "He was kind and noble, and I suspect among the wisest of his kind. I say suspect because sphinxes are famously private, but Hakor—and Bek, because of Hakor . . . They always had time to talk to me . . . and to let me pose riddles that must have seemed like child's play to them. And now—unless we can do something about it—noble, kind Hakor will be petrified forever."

The elevator was quiet.

Well, for one floor. Then it said, "No wonder you're all so very upset. Why, it makes me want to weep just to think of such an ancient, dignified creature turning to stone!"

The elevator did, in fact, sound like it was upset. Could an elevator cry?

But then Stephen saw something even more troubling. A tear slid down Ivan's cheek, just as the elevator doors opened on to the Village. Ivan rushed out onto the green. "I'll see you later," he said. "Don't follow me."

Sofia pulled on Stephen's arm to hold him back. "Let him go—I'm sure he needs a little time to himself, then he'll be ready. Ivan doesn't like anyone seeing him cry."

"How thoughtless of me!" the elevator said. "It was what I said, wasn't it? But I meant it!"

"It's okay, Elevator," Stephen said. "It's been a rough day, that's all."

"I can understand rough days. That I can," said the elevator, and its doors closed with a soft, "Sleep well."

Sofia and Stephen stepped out onto the green. Across the way, Ivan had almost made it to his cottage. The lights were on inside, so his parents must be home; maybe working on the Edmund case. Maybe they knew what to say to make Ivan feel better.

"It's like Dad said: 'Tomorrow will be better,'" Sofia said. But she didn't sound like she entirely believed it.

"I hope so," Stephen said.

He didn't sound like he believed it either.

Stephen decided not to wait up for his dad after finishing his pizza. But he didn't fall asleep right away either. He couldn't stop thinking of Bek's cries of anguish. No wonder Ivan was so upset. Ivan had known Hakor even longer than Bek had. Stephen pulled *An Almanack of the Mores and Ways of Supernormal Kind* out of his nightstand drawer and thumbed through the pages until he came to the entry on sphinxes. Sure, it was unlikely he'd find anything about how to unpetrify Hakor, but he couldn't stand sitting around doing nothing, not when Ivan was clearly so worried. There must be *some* way they could help.

Native to the dry regions of North Africa and the Levant, sphinxes have served as guardians of secret and secure places since before the beginning of recorded supernormal history. The most commonly appearing variety of sphinx has the head of a human being, the body of a lion, and the wings of an eagle, but other forms are known to exist; some capable of flight and some not.

That was interesting. And they were both furred and feathered. Stephen wondered whether the current Octagon representative for the sphinxes was Trevor's mom or that cranky firebird who didn't like Cindermass.

A loud crunching sound in the garden outside drifted through Stephen's round porthole-like bedroom window. It was cracked open at the bottom to let in the warm night air. Looking over, he couldn't see anything but his own reflection and a sliver of darkness, so he turned off his bedside lamp.

As soon as the light went out, another crash sounded, and Stephen heard a voice he recognized.

"Move over!" Ivan said. "You're crushing me against the fence!"

Another crash, then it was Sofia's voice. "Now *you're* crushing the rosebushes! Just stay still for a minute, okay?"

There was a muffled response from a third voice,

and by then, Stephen was up and across the room, opening the window the rest of the way. In the dim light, he saw his two friends flanking Bek. The sphinx saw him before either Ivan or Sofia did.

"Hurry, Stephen Lawson," she said. "I have left my post, risking my position, to visit you three here."

"Why?" Stephen asked.

"I sent for her," Ivan said. "By gargoyle."

"Your note said you wanted to save Hakor," Bek said.

"First, we need you to tell us if it's possible," Ivan said. "Stephen, come out. We need to talk."

CHAPTER SEVEN

Stephen blinked down at the trio. "You can come in if you want—Dad's not back yet."

Bek stretched out her wings. "I can't fit through your human-size door," she said. "Even with these furled tight."

Fair enough.

"Be right there." Stephen shut the window and hurried through the cottage to the front door. He found Sofia, Ivan, and Bek waiting out front.

"Gazebo?" Sofia said.

"Let's go," Ivan said. "The gargoyles promised me they would be discreet."

"I can't stay long," Bek said. "I'm not truly allowed to leave my post. But my new mentor hasn't arrived yet."

She loped along beside the three kids. Just as they approached the gazebo on the village lawn where the croquet matches were usually held—unless the mallets and balls had been stolen by rogue monkeys—two shapes darted down from the sky and landed in front of them.

"Sollie, Liz," Sofia said, "you almost gave me a heart attack. I thought you were being discreet."

Sollie and Liz folded their hands in front of their stocky bodies. Liz spoke. "We wanted to speak to Bekhetamun. Art said he neglected to express our sympathies when he delivered your missive. So, we wanted to do so, on behalf of the entire family. Gargoyles know all too well the pain of a wizard turning a loved one to stone."

Stephen had no idea what they were talking about on the gargoyle side—he'd have to ask Ivan later. . . .

A frown made deep lines in Sollie's face. "We are so very, very sorry. Have you been relieved of your assignment? We would gladly harbor you. You could work with us."

"Thank you, Granite Mountain Clan." Bek accepted their condolences and the job offer with a nod. "That's not why I'm here, though. Ivan wanted to see me. Will you give us privacy?"

"And you won't mention Bek being here?" Sofia added. "Ivan said you promised. We need to keep this meeting quiet for her sake."

"Whatever we can do," Liz said, steering Sollie away.

So, they could probably count on the gargoyles not ratting them out to their parents. Speaking of which . . . "Are your parents home, Ivan?" Stephen asked.

He shook his head. "They left to begin work on the case of the infamous Edmund the Enchanter. I'm sleeping over at Sofia's."

"My folks aren't home yet," she said.

"But they will be, probably about the same time as my dad," Stephen said. He pulled his phone and consulted it. After eleven. "We've got maybe half an hour."

"Then we'd better get started," Ivan said.

The four of them crowded into the gazebo on the lawn. Even though she was much smaller than Hakor, Bek was large enough that her hindquarters still stuck out one side of the wooden structure as she lay on her belly.

"What do you need to know?" she asked.

Ivan's lips tightened. "First, what are the rules governing a sphinx's petrification?"

Bek frowned. "The High Rules of Riddles apply in this situation. They are the binding laws of sphinxkind. The first one states that if sphinxes ever fail in their charge of guardianship by being bested in a contest of riddles, then they shall be permanently petrified."

Stephen's spirits sank. "That doesn't sound great."

It sounded, well, *permanent*.

Sofia leaned forward. "What are the rest? Are they about petrification, too?"

"Excellent questions," Ivan said.

"There is one other rule about petrification," Bek said. "It was added after the Great Sphinx's petrification. That rule says that *if* it can be *proven* that the riddle was answered by devious or underhanded means, then the petrification will be reversed. It also says mentors can undo petrification of their apprentices in circumstances when they deem it warranted. If only I'd had a riddle of my own. I wish Hakor hadn't had to give his."

Bek sounded miserable, but Ivan sat bolt upright. He said, "Bek, I asked you to come because I believe Edmund the Enchanter cheated. I didn't want to give you false hope. But I now have real hope that Hakor can be revived."

Bek gasped. Her feathers ruffled. "There's no other way Edmund could've cracked that riddle in time! Do you have evidence?"

Ivan took out his notebook and a shiny gold pen. "Not yet," Ivan said. "Only my detective's keen intuition and powers of observation."

Bek deflated. "That won't matter. We need real evidence."

Ivan had his fingers at his chin, the gold pen clasped there. It was one of his thinking postures. Thinking was Ivan's favorite thing to do—although a close second would be spraying people with the unusual substances that he kept in his many hidden pockets specifically for the purpose of detection. This was a good sign.

It cheered Stephen up, and he said, "Don't worry, we'll get it."

"But will the Octagon listen to you?" Bek asked.

"The Octagon is too busy to worry about Hakor," Ivan said, lowering his hand. "That's why we must handle this investigation. I won't lie to you: this is the hardest case I have ever encountered. But we will get the proof and make them listen. I will not shrink from the challenge."

Tears glistened in her eyes. "Ivanos, I know you are up to this task. Hakor trusted you completely."

Stephen's heart pounded. "What do we have to do now?"

"First things first," Ivan said. "How could someone sneak into the Grove of Memory, now that it is closed to outsiders?"

"Can someone explain this grove to me?" Stephen asked. "I don't understand why it's the only way to cheat."

Bek was silent for a long moment. "The grove is a sacred and secret place that only the leaders of our people can choose to share with an outsider, and they have chosen not to for thousands of years. For me to tell you details would be to break one of the High Rules, as well. I can confirm only what everyone knows: that it is where the answers to our riddles are kept."

That wasn't completely useless, and Stephen understood why she couldn't say more. But it was frustrating.

"Now," Ivan said, "what would constitute proof that Edmund penetrated the grove's security and solved the riddle through devious or underhanded means?"

Bek growled as she considered. "Anything that proves he accessed the Grove of Memory should work."

"Hmm." Ivan mulled this.

Stephen thought it was a little vague, but workable. Right?

"We've got this, haven't we?" Sofia asked.

"We'll make do. Criminals leave evidence, and so, Edmund must have left some as well. Bek," Ivan said, "I have one more question: Had you ever seen Edmund before he asked for the riddle?"

The sphinx girl shook her head vehemently. "Not that I remember."

"Ah, that's the rub. We've learned that a spell makes him difficult to notice," Ivan said. "So, I will need to hypnotize you to be sure you're correct. It might be a clue we can use."

"I thought hypnotism was fake," Stephen said.

"Not when great detectives practice it," Ivan said, reaching into his pocket and drawing out another ink pen. "This is a special Pen of Mesmerism."

"What do I do?" Bek asked.

Ivan lifted his pen and held it in front of her face. It had a little light at the end of it. "Focus on this object and the sound of my voice."

Bek stared at the pen as Ivan swung it slowly back and forth. "Relax, Bekhetamun. Keep watching the movement of the pen, the light."

Stephen and Sofia sat forward, watching.

Stephen was afraid to make a sound.

"Close your eyes," Ivan said. "And picture Edmund. The feathered hat, the cloak . . ."

Her eyes closed, and that growling noise sounded in her throat.

"Go back past today, back, back . . . Now I want you to picture the area around your plinth, and scan for Edmund. If you see him, zero in on the image, and we'll determine when it is."

It only took a moment. "I see him!"

"Good," Ivan said. "Do you know when it was?"

This pause lasted longer, with Bek murmuring and moving her head, as if watching a silent movie behind her eyelids. At last, she opened her eyes. Then she blinked. "Should I have asked before I opened my eyes?"

"That's fine," Ivan said. "Do you know when you first saw him?"

"Some months ago. That was the only time until today. He was in a crowd on the sidewalk. He was talking to himself."

Ivan made notes with the Pen of Mesmerism,

which apparently also doubled as a normal pen.

"What does it mean?" Bek asked.

"That his plan—which we shall uncover—has been in the works for at least a few months." Ivan pushed his glasses up on his nose. "Bek, I want nothing more than to say that I'm certain the training I have undergone, and the knowledge I have absorbed, will be enough to prove that Edmund the Enchanter is a fiend, and to restore Hakor to life. Our foe is obviously crafty, if he managed to cheat a sphinx and not be caught immediately. But if there is any way to prove his treachery, we will."

Stephen thought he knew what Ivan needed to hear. What they all did. "We're going to do our best. Because you, Ivan, are a great friend. You managed to help me when the Court of Thorns was against us. You wouldn't give up, even when you might have been lost to Faery, too. I may be new here, but I know if anyone can do this, it's the three of us together."

Ivan inclined his head and gave a slight smile. "We will vanquish this foe together."

"Together," Sofia said.

The sphinx dove forward, pulling all three of them into a hug, her wings folded around him. Her fur was soft against Stephen's cheek.

"Thank you," she said. "Thank you all."

"You'd best get back," Ivan said quietly, "before someone else realizes you're here."

"Yes," Bek said.

She released them and backed out of the gazebo. When she spread her wings wide, they shimmered in the dark. "Thank you," she said again, and with a mighty leap she disappeared into the night sky. This afternoon, Stephen had thought of her as a kid like them, but she seemed to have aged years since then.

"This is good," Stephen said. "We'll save Hakor."

"Yes, we will." Sofia's response was soft.

"If not, we'll be responsible for breaking Bek's heart, too," Ivan said. "But you're right. The three of us are a formidable force. Edmund will be busy with the Octagon's investigation into his evil plot. He'll never see us coming."

CHAPTER EIGHT

His dad had cheesy scrambled eggs and sourdough toast on the table when Stephen wandered into their cozy kitchen the next morning. Stephen hadn't even bothered to change out of his pajamas yet.

His dad looked up from the table, where he'd been reading something on the tablet next to his plate.

"Whew," he said. "Thought I lost my touch there, and your eggs were going to get cold."

Stephen didn't know if it was a chef thing or a his-dad thing, or maybe both, but it was true that his dad always managed to have breakfast ready at the perfect time.

"Sorry," Stephen said, and scrubbed a hand through his hair. He sat down at the table and picked up his toast, already glistening with a light coating of butter. "Yesterday was a long day. I guess I slept late."

He took a bite, thinking about Ivan's pronouncement from the night before that they might break Bek's heart. Would they be able to save Hakor?

They'd just have to figure it out. Stephen believed in what he'd said. The three of them together could do just about anything.

"You probably needed the rest." Stephen's dad got up to take his own plate to the sink. "You have dinner with your mom tonight?" He asked it casually, although there was nothing casual about Stephen finally getting to know his mother. He and his dad hadn't talked about her that much since she'd returned. It was still so new to have her in their lives. In fact, their whole lives here at the New Harmonia were still new.

"Yeah." Stephen crunched a bite of toast. "Unless Octagon business takes precedence, I guess. It was pretty strange seeing her there with all the rest of them yesterday."

"Something tells me your mother won't let any business intrude." He finished rinsing his dishes and then turned back to face Stephen. "She treasures your time together."

"Did she say that?" Stephen tried to keep his voice casual, too.

His dad laughed. "She did. She also said you're getting much better at your fae animation—you'll have to show me."

"We're working on a painting together," Stephen said, finishing up his eggs.

He thought the painting was turning out pretty well, but he was also afraid he wasn't much of an impartial judge. It was the first painting he'd ever done with his mother, and so *of course* he thought it was good.

"And you're having fun getting to know her?" his dad asked.

"I am. Sometimes I still feel nervous around her. It's hard to forget she's, you know, a fae princess."

His dad laid a hand on Stephen's shoulder and scooped up his now empty plate with the other. "Tell me about it. So, what are you up to today?"

The question came at the exact same moment as a knock at the door. Before either of them could answer it, the door swung open to reveal Ivan and Sofia. They rushed in, and Sofia shouted, "Go away, monkeys! No croquet for you today!" before slamming it shut.

"Good morning," his dad said. "I guess that answers my question. You're hanging out with your friends today."

Ivan was peering at Stephen with his glasses down his nose. "You're not even dressed," he said.

Sofia cleared her throat. "Hi, Chef Lawson."

Ivan shook his head and gave a half bow. "Good

morning, Chef. Sorry, I forgot my manners." Then he fixed his stare back on Stephen. "We've got a lot to do today."

Stephen's dad had one of those knowing smiles adults wore when they thought they knew everything about what kids were going to get up to.

You have no idea, Stephen thought. And then: *I have no idea.*

Where would they even get started trying to prove Edmund had cheated? They'd have to do that if they were going to bring Hakor back to life.

Sofia wore a somber-for-her gray dress with her black boots. In contrast, Stephen had never seen Ivan in such a colorful suit. Brown tweed by the look of it, but threaded through with oranges and reds. A bizarre choice for a broiling city summer. Which meant it was likely filled with even more extra pockets than usual for detective gear.

"Are you going to get changed, or are you wearing your pajamas?" Ivan asked.

Stephen pushed his chair back and headed toward his room. "Be right back," he said.

"I'm timing you!" Ivan called.

"He really is," Sofia put in. "He just whipped out a stopwatch. So, hurry!"

Stephen heard his dad laugh again.

The elevator opened the second Stephen's finger hovered over the button. "Hurry up!" the elevator said.

The three of them looked at one another, then shrugged and got on.

"What's up, Elevator?" Stephen asked.

"For once I, wretched as I am, have news! As you know, most of what I hear is so boring. People bragging about walking here or riding in a taxi there— They are so uncouth! Don't they realize it's just rubbing in my face that I will never leave this simple shaft?" The elevator paused to sigh. "No, my days and nights are up and down, basement to the Village. That's life for me. While everyone else gets surprises and . . . to go outside! People have no sense of how lucky they are, especially supernormals, who can go anywhere with just a few steps through a gateway."

The elevator zinged down without stopping at any of the floors, and Stephen thought they might not have time to find out what the supposed news was.

"Not me," Stephen said truthfully. He couldn't use the lobby gateways because his half-fae nature made it too dangerous.

"Of course not you!" the elevator cried. "You would never be so *rude*."

Ivan raised his eyebrows and kept them there. Sofia tapped the side of Stephen's sneaker with her boot.

"Elevator, what's your news?" Stephen asked, just as they stopped at the lobby. The doors opened with a *bing*!

"Oh! Just that Edmund the Enchanter is moving into the hotel! I'm to be free to carry him and his things, so you might have to wait for me at some point today. I just wanted you to know why. Normally I prioritize you above all."

What? Stephen could guess his friends felt the same way he did. As if they'd stepped into a parallel dimension.

"Ugh," the elevator said, apparently unaware of the size of the bombshell it had just dropped. "Mad scientist on nine calling. I'd better go." It let out a heavy sigh, and that was their cue to step out. Then the elevator was gone.

"It can't be true, can it?" Stephen asked. "And why would he be a priority?"

Sofia waved her hand in front of them. "Well, something's up."

"Indeed." Ivan scrutinized the flurry of activity in the lobby.

This was busier than the busiest days Stephen had seen so far—and according to Ivan and Sofia, summer was peak vacation season for supernormals, just like humans. Carmen was scowling into a phone, making notes as she talked. The desk clerks were scurrying around behind the registration counter, helping a line of supernormals that ranged from minotaurs to dwarves to mermaids. In fact, there were just *more* people than usual everywhere.

As they took in the bustling scene, the tiny, rude Sigmund Dormouse strutted through the front doors with Madame Veronika behind him. "Make way!" he shouted, brandishing a miniature megaphone that worked like a charm. Maybe it *was* a charm, Stephen thought.

"What is going on?" Stephen asked. "Why are *they* here?"

Ivan turned and pushed his glasses up on his nose. "I think we all know who can answer that most efficiently."

"Cindermass," Stephen and Sofia said in chorus.

Cindermass was the dragon who served as the hotel's backup heating—and primary gossip—system. He also happened to have been Stephen's late grandmother's dearest friend.

Ivan nodded and walked briskly to the stairwell that led down to Cindermass's lair. "I'd planned to start with Cindermass anyway, after Chenghiz brought him up yesterday."

Stephen found the torches in the dark at the top of the stairs and distributed them to his friends. Sofia lit the long-handled lighter that always waited there, and the cloths at the ends of their torches flared into bright flame. Down and down the long stone stairs they went with their flickering lights, Ivan in the lead.

Finally they reached the big double doors at the bottom of the stairs. Which were already open.

"Curious," Ivan said.

The dragon laughed in what sounded like utter delight, but they couldn't see either Cindermass or the reason for his mirth from where they stood.

"And curiouser," Sofia agreed. "He must be entertaining."

"Huh," Stephen said. He placed his torch in a sconce beside the open doors, noting that there was already a torch in the one beside it, and waited for his friends to do the same. He hesitated. "We're not breaking some ancient code by interrupting, are we?"

Sofia considered, her head tilting to one side. But it was Ivan who answered dryly, "I guess we'll know if he decides to set us on fire. You're his favorite; you go first."

Although Stephen *knew* Cindermass would never

do such a thing, it still wasn't an image he wanted to dwell on. Still . . . "Okay, I'll chance it," he said, and stepped forward.

Ivan and Sofia followed suit and—like Stephen—stopped after a few feet.

There were the familiar sights of Cindermass's lair, illuminated by more torches: Piles of coins that reached nearly to the ceiling. The dragon's prized collection of paintings (including a portrait by Stephen) and statues, suits of armor, and other fabulous displays of wealth that filled the enormous room.

And obviously the giant red dragon himself. He lounged in front of the tallest pile of his hoard.

Across from him was . . .

Edmund the Enchanter. He sat at complete ease at the tea table where Stephen, Ivan, and Sofia usually sat, his feet out to one side and crossed at the ankles. He wore the same outlandish hat as the day before, a purple silk shirt, and his flashy cloak.

"It looks very well on you," he said to Cindermass. "Almost as if it were created just for you to wear it— Why else are there gems if not for dragons to enjoy them, eh?"

"You've been reading the great draconic natural histories, I see," Cindermass said, delighted. "As far as dragonkind is concerned, there is no other reason."

Stephen shook his head at Ivan and Sofia. He half expected they'd need to turn tail and get back to the lobby immediately. But Ivan's shoulders were set in a straight line. The boy detective marched forward.

"Cindermass," Ivan said, "what are you doing?"

"Ivan!" Cindermass grinned a toothy smile, his hand at his throat. "Sofia! And my dear Stephen! You must come and meet my charming new friend."

Edmund looked over at them, his eyes widening in a moment's surprise before he smirked.

"We've met," Stephen said.

"You have?" Cindermass asked. Then he spoke to Edmund. "But you said that *I* was your first important social call once you decided on your new position."

Ha, Stephen thought. *Now you get to see what an offended dragon can do. And what new position?*

"Oh you are," Edmund said. "I have met these three, but before I took on my new role. I didn't even realize they were friends of yours. That would have made them *much* more important."

The dragon relaxed, satisfied with that answer. "True."

Cindermass still had a claw to his throat, though, as if he were holding something there. A necklace of some sort. Then again, he *loved* jewelry.

"At any rate," Cindermass said, and waved his free claw, "do come in. You three simply *must* admire my new gift. A belated birthday present from Edmund!"

"We'd love to," Sofia said, stomping forward.

When they reached the table, Stephen had no doubt that Sofia purposely stationed herself between Edmund and Ivan. He carefully took a seat on the far side.

Edmund continued to smirk as Ivan glared at him. He couldn't even be bothered to sit up straight, instead lounging as if he belonged there as much as Cindermass. Which he did not. Why on earth would the Manager let Edmund move into the hotel when the Octagon was investigating him?

It must be a trap. Madame Veronika had been upstairs, after all.

That possibility was mildly comforting.

"Can we see the gift?" Stephen asked, facing Cindermass. He didn't want to look in the enchanter's smug face any longer.

Cindermass preened, caressing with razor-sharp talons the gold chain that hung around his neck. At last, he removed his claw to reveal the showpiece in full.

A shimmering blue sphere the size of a basketball dangled from the center of the chain.

"Isn't it just lovely?" he said, fluttering his golden eyes. "Isn't it just divine?"

Stephen knew better than to say anything that Cindermass might interpret as criticism of any of his treasures—whether or not Stephen thought the item in question was tacky and from an unseemly source. So, he said, "It certainly is. Is it a real crystal ball?"

Cindermass drew back. "Of the highest quality! Though I won't be using it for anything so mundane as peering through space and time to read the past or tell the future."

"Of course not," said Sofia. "That would be entirely too ordinary for a being as magnificent as yourself."

Anyone else might think that Sofia was being sarcastic—and maybe she was, at least a little bit—but Cindermass just preened all the more.

"Yes, yes," he said. "Leave such conjurings and weavings for the witches and sorcerers like dear Edmund here, I say. This bauble serves a *much* better purpose now, don't you think?"

Stephen hesitated to ask, but decided to risk it. "What purpose is that, Cindermass?"

"Why, setting off my eyes, of course! Don't you think the blue makes the orange rims around my irises just pop?"

As an artist, Stephen studied things like this.

And the particular shade of blue glowing from the crystal, and the fiery shade of orange glowing from Cindermass's eyes, didn't, in his opinion, actually go well together at all. He also didn't believe that Edmund would give Cindermass this ugly jewel just to be nice.

"Yes," said Stephen. "Your eyes definitely pop."

He looked over his shoulder to find Ivan's attention finally leaving Edmund. Ivan blinked at the crystal ball, then stared intently at it. Some people might have said he was being rude.

Not Cindermass, though. "Ivan, you clearly appreciate the quality of my newest acquisition," he said.

"Appreciate?" Ivan asked. "Yes, I suppose. I'm curious about it, certainly. It's the Sphere of Crystal Vision, isn't it?"

"Indeed," Cindermass said, grinning with pleasure. "One of a kind." He chuckled, tendrils of steam emerging from his nostrils. "Like myself."

"But what can it do?" Stephen asked.

Edmund uncrossed his ankles and sat forward.

"A fine question. What can it do? What *can* it *do*?" Edmund clearly loved hearing himself talk. "What it can do depends largely upon the holder. It is a beautiful ornamentation, as you see. Or it can be used by a sorcerer or witch to behold another time and place."

Ivan's hands were at his sides, and almost balled into fists. Almost. Sofia stood up.

"Convenient that you just happened to have such an item and then not need it any longer," Ivan said. Then he added, "Though I suppose none of us should be surprised. Given that you are a cheater."

So much for Edmund not seeing them coming.

CHAPTER NINE

Cindermass extended his neck to its full height, and smoke streamed out of his nose.

"Ivanos La Doyt," the dragon said, "you should be extremely careful in insulting an honored guest to *my* hoard. What do you mean by making such a wild accusation?" He stroked a claw over the all-seeing disco ball around his neck. "Apologize to Edmund right now."

Edmund shifted the folds of his cloak to reveal the crescent wand hanging from a belt loop at his side. "Yes," Edmund said, with a sharp laugh. "Why would someone as accomplished as I need to cheat at anything?"

"Cindermass, are you going to let him threaten us?" Stephen asked, disbelieving.

"I hear no threat, Stephen," the dragon said. "Only a question that seems fair, given Ivan's outburst. It seems you three have gotten off on the wrong foot with Edmund. He's an important figure in the supernormal community—"

"What are you talking about?" Sofia cut in. "And is your goodwill really for purchase with a crystal necklace?"

Flame flared in Cindermass's gaping mouth as he

reared back. The temperature in the room increased by at least ten degrees in an instant.

Usually Sofia was their protector, but Stephen felt like he had the best chance of calming Cindermass down. "Cindermass . . ." He searched for what to say. "We can explain."

The dragon's eyes glowed at him. Then Cindermass focused on Edmund. "I am so very sorry for this . . . scene." He waved his talons to Stephen, Ivan, and Sofia. "Explain, then."

"Well," Stephen started, but Ivan held up a hand to speak.

"Cindermass," Ivan said slowly, his first words since his accusation, "why do you think Edmund gave you that gift?"

Cindermass blinked his glowing eyes. "Because . . . I am me!"

"It's interesting," Ivan said. "Yesterday, we were called before the Octagon to report on the events we witnessed involving your new friend. Namely his using some underhanded technique in order to answer Hakor's riddle correctly and get that wand he just flashed at us. Now here he is, apparently having declared he's moving into the hotel. Everyone is going along with it—which I don't understand at all!"

"Ivan!" Cindermass protested, a claw to his chest. "You go too far!"

Ivan obviously didn't think so. "And then he gives you a priceless gift. The Octagon is looking into whatever he's up to, and as you—and Edmund—know, Chenghiz would love to believe you're involved."

"Do not mention that foul firebird's name in my lair!" The temperature in the room approached boiling. Cindermass said, "Edmund, is any of this true?"

Edmund stood. He peered down at Ivan, who didn't shrink from him. There was something like respect in Edmund's eyes, and then he turned to Cindermass. "Of course it isn't true," Edmund said soothingly. "Why don't *I* explain?"

He began to do the same exact thing he'd done the day before: he paced and expounded. "I met these three at the Cabinet of Wonders yesterday, because I was there after I answered Hakor the sphinx's riddle. The rest of this boy's theory is pure fabrication. I imagine he has no way to prove any of his outlandish charges." Edmund paused and waited for an objection.

Ivan's fingers *were* curled into fists now. Sofia placed a hand on his arm.

"As I thought," Edmund said. "Hakor asked a riddle. I answered within the time allotted. I collected my prize from within the Cabinet. I had a special social call I wanted to make, now that I was in the city. Seeing as we did not meet in time for your birthday, and given the rules about a birthday being the rare time one such as yourself can add to a horde . . . Well, giving you the sphere felt entirely fitting. I have always had difficulty finding intellectual peers. It is not every day one meets a dragon with the wisdom of a thousand years."

Cindermass let out a long exhale of smoke. "No, it is not. You see, children? Edmund has cleared all of this up, as I knew he would. Now, Edmund, would you mind leaving me alone with these three? I need to have a word with them about their behavior."

Edmund hesitated. "But . . . Not at all." He winked at them. "I'm sure I'll be seeing you three fascinating young people again very *soon*. And you, of course, Cindermass."

"Of course," Cindermass agreed. "We are to be great friends."

The enchanter nodded to Cindermass, then strode out of the lair.

"You sent him away so we could talk openly?" Ivan asked, once Edmund was gone.

Cindermass blinked. His golden eyes continued to glow. "No, Ivanos," Cindermass said. "I sent him away to reiterate what I said before: I will not have my guest—a friend of mine—disrespected."

Stephen couldn't believe this. "Cindermass, *we're* your friends."

The dragon's big head shook heavily from side to side. "Which is why I have to tell you when your behavior embarrasses me."

"Cindermass, what is going on?" Sofia asked.

"I don't know what you mean," the dragon said.

"Oh," Ivan muttered. Raising his voice, he said, "Stephen, Sofia . . ." He clasped his hands contritely in front of himself. "Cindermass is right."

Stephen did a double take. Had he heard Ivan correctly? "He is?"

The dragon huffed. "Of course I am."

"We were out of line," Ivan said, ignoring Stephen in favor of Cindermass. "Obviously Edmund *is* a friend to you, or why would he have given you such a gift? I let my zest for detection get ahead of me."

Cindermass nodded his giant head. "We all make mistakes." He paused. "Except me."

Yeah, Stephen thought. *Befriending an evil sorcerer isn't a mistake at all.* Was Cindermass already under some sort of spell? They had until the crescent moon, right? And what was up with Ivan's about-face?

"We should be on our way," Ivan said deliberately, raising his eyebrows at Stephen and Sofia. At least maybe they'd soon find out what *he* was thinking. "We need to catch up to Edmund and apologize."

"If you say so," Sofia said, sounding as confused as Stephen felt. But she started to back out of the room with a wave to Cindermass.

Stephen still had another question for the dragon. "You said something about Edmund's new position before? What position is it?"

Cindermass grinned a toothy grin. He loved knowing more than others. "Why, he's to be king."

"King of what?" Stephen asked, puzzled.

"Everything," Cindermass said, smoke wafting from between his giant teeth. "Edmund is soon to be the king of all supernormalkind. It's very exciting. He asked me to be one of his advisers." The disco ball of time around his neck flashed. "He was so generous to give you an audience, even after Ivan's rude remarks. Don't you think he'll make a wonderful ruler?"

Cindermass couldn't *really* think that was a good idea, could he?

"I guess we'll find out," Stephen said, following his friends in their hasty retreat.

* * *

Stephen waited until they were on the stairs, well away from the lair, before he spoke. "Ivan, would you like to share what is going on?"

"Yes," Sofia agreed. "What am I missing?"

"A great deal, mostly likely," Ivan said, holding his torch higher.

"Ha," Stephen said.

"Ha-ha," Sofia said. "Now tell us what you mean."

Ivan stopped on the stairs and turned to face them, the flicker of the torch flames reflecting on the lenses of his glasses. "It's simple— No, it's entirely complex."

Sofia let out a frustrated moan. "Spit. It. Out."

"Is Cindermass brainwashed?" Stephen asked.

"Not brainwashed," Ivan said. "He's been whammied—victim of the wand's effect, assuming I'm correct. I posit that Madame Veronika's wording when she spoke of the wand has a greater magical meaning. Remember how she said 'when used during a specific crescent moon cycle'?"

"Yes," Stephen said. "But don't we also have three more days?"

"Two now," Ivan responded. "We can assume that the cycle is already in progress. And remember how he spoke in a language we couldn't understand at the Cabinet? He could have started to enact his plan right then . . . by casting—or beginning the casting—of a spell."

"Which is to become king," Stephen said. "But—"

"If it's a spell, why aren't we affected?" Sofia asked.

"That, I don't know. Yet." Ivan faced forward again and started up the stairs. "I want to observe Edmund interacting with others in the hotel if we can."

"I don't particularly want to get whammied," Stephen said.

"Avoid mind control," Ivan said. "Good plan. We will observe *from a distance*. I fear we would soon forget our mission and our promise to Bek if we were to fall under Edmund's influence."

They started up the stairs again.

"Can he really declare himself king?" Stephen asked, cold running through him despite the torch in his hand.

"Signs point to yes," Ivan said. "But he won't. Or at least not for long. While we work on proving he cheated, the Octagon will figure out how to thwart him. Hakor will be returned to life and Edmund's plan will be unsuccessful."

"I like the sound of that much better than King Talks-A-Lot," Sofia said.

Stephen didn't know that much about supernormal society yet, but . . . "I didn't think there was royalty in that sense anyway. I thought the Octagon ruled over everything."

"They do. But if someone could *make* them to do his bidding . . ." Ivan allowed Stephen to draw his own conclusion.

Ivan continued as they marched up the stairs toward the lobby. "I also want to do some research on the Sphere of Crystal Vision. Edmund *must* have used it in his cheating scheme somehow. We should consult with the visiting scholar in the library."

"There's a visiting scholar in the library?" Stephen hadn't heard anything about that.

"Got here yesterday," Sofia said. "He's cute."

"Cute?" Ivan said, offended. "Only you would describe one of the foremost scholarly minds on the planet as cute."

"Well, he is."

"Who is—" Stephen started to ask, but Ivan raised his hand for quiet. There were voices on the other side of the door in the lobby.

Quickly they snuffed out their torches, and as soon as they were all ready, Sofia gingerly eased the door open. They emerged to find quite a scene. Beside a gateway showing a big old stone manse and a field of heather were Madame Veronika and Jersey Pete, Sigmund Dormouse, and Sofia's mother. Edmund was also there, along with a man who was plainly related to him. They had the same dark hair, the same broad forehead, the same haughty air.

What they did not share was fashion sense. Where Edmund cut a colorful figure, his relative wore a long, plain black cloak. Expensive and classy-looking.

Sofia steered Ivan and Stephen close to the shadows along the wall. "They said they wanted to interview his family yesterday."

For the first time, Edmund didn't seem calm and cool. His cheeks were flushed, and his eyes narrowed.

He's angry, Stephen thought. *Or no, upset about something.*

The man who looked like Edmund shook his head and curled his lip in disgust. "Well done, Edmund. You've caused the Octagon to interrupt a chess match just when I'd called checkmate on that reptilian loser your cousin married. And for what? So I can tell Madame Veronika"—he said the name almost sarcastically—"that no one has used the clockwork sundial of late. I checked. And that *I* know nothing of whatever ridiculous scheme you're attempting."

"Uncle," Edmund said, "I think it's time you treated me with greater respect."

Edmund sounded a little plaintive and almost . . . sad. Stephen barely recognized his voice; it was so different from his usual boasting.

"Yes, Elliot Darkfell," Sofia's mom said. "I must

insist you treat the most honored guest in the hotel in the manner he deserves."

"Mom's been whammied, too?" Sofia whispered in dismay.

"It appears so," Ivan said, quietly.

Elliot frowned in confusion. Edmund smiled at Carmen, though, and flung back one shoulder of his cloak to put his hand on the wand at his side. "Thank you, Lady Diplomatis. I would also like to know on what basis the Octagon is investigating my actions."

Madame Veronika held up her hand. "Edmund, the wand is yours, but the Octagon would like to know what you intend to do with it. We'd encourage you to let cooler heads prevail here. Let's discuss this rationally."

So, Madame Veronika wasn't as susceptible to Edmund's charm spell as everyone else either. That was one good thing.

"Good luck!" Elliot Darkfell said dismissively.

"I'm afraid my uncle is correct on this matter. Rationality and cool heads aren't things our family does very well," Edmund said. He took the wand off his belt and held it in his right hand. His fingers gripped it hard, knuckles pale with the pressure. "Especially not Uncle Elliot."

"Edmund, it's hardly my fault you decided to spell yourself into obscurity at thirteen," Elliot countered. "What were we supposed to do? No one noticed you even after you started dressing like some runaway from the circus."

"They notice me now," Edmund said, sweeping the wand around to indicate Carmen and Madame Veronika. "And so will you."

"What in Hades's name are you talking about?" Elliot smirked.

Edmund's cloak swished as he took a step forward. "Once the crescent moon rises tomorrow night, my name will live *forever* in legend. *I* will be head of the family—the head of everything— just as I should have been groomed to be from the start."

"Here we go," Elliot said, rolling his eyes. "Delusions of grandeur."

Edmund smiled a slow, cool smile. "Lady Diplomatis, are my accommodations ready?"

Carmen eagerly stepped up. "Yes, the Manager has designed your suite on the twelfth floor exactly as directed. The gargoyles delivered your belongings there a short while ago."

"I'd like rooms for my uncle, too," Edmund said. "On a much lower floor."

"Right away," Carmen said.

"I'm not staying." Elliot sniffed. "Not to watch this pathetic performance."

"I'll show you a pathetic performance tomorrow evening," Edmund said. Then he grimaced, as he apparently realized it wasn't much of a comeback. He extended the wand toward his uncle. "You are staying. You will remain here until I tell you that you can go home. Understood?"

When Elliot answered, the words came out forced. "My pleasure."

"I thought so." Edmund replaced the wand on his belt.

"Edmund, can I have a word?" Madame Veronika

tried again. Jersey Pete even stepped in front of him. "Perhaps in private?"

"Make an appointment. I have no need to talk to the Octagon . . . yet."

Sofia tugged on Stephen's shirt and Ivan's jacket sleeve. "Let's go before he sees us," she said.

She darted over to the door to the upstairs and ushered them through just as Edmund's cloak swished in their direction.

CHAPTER
TEN

They didn't stop until they reached the third-floor landing.

"He didn't see us, did he?" Stephen peered down to see if anyone was behind them. He was relieved not to see a figure in a whooshing cloak giving chase up the stairs.

"I don't think so." Sofia pushed the door to the third floor open.

They started up the long hallway lined with doors. The hotel's library was one of the first places Ivan and Sofia had brought Stephen after he moved into the New Harmonia. Ivan and libraries had a mutual affection for each other, from what Stephen could tell.

"Why is it just us and Madame Veronika who seem unaffected?" Stephen asked.

"He did have to use the wand on his uncle," Ivan said, frowning. "Maybe people here aren't affected, unless he targets them directly."

"I can't believe he got to Mom," Sofia said.

"It'll be all right," Ivan told her. "It has to be."

Stephen crossed his fingers that Ivan was correct.

"It's weird," Stephen said. "Why is he setting himself up here at the hotel and being so out in the open? Wouldn't it be smarter to *hide* until after the crescent moon?"

"Ah," Ivan said. "But he accidentally spelled himself; he's been in hiding of sorts for years. He must not be able to help himself now that everyone can see him."

"Yeah," Sofia put in. "He wants everyone to see how great he and his big plans are."

That did seem true. "And his outfits," Stephen said.

Stephen almost felt sympathetic toward Edmund . . . at least a little bit. It would be terrible to be essentially invisible, to have everyone ignore you for most of your life—even if it was your own fault. And based on his uncle Elliot, Edmund's family didn't exactly seem loving and supportive.

But then again, Edmund also behaved like a colossal jerk himself.

"Here we are." Ivan stopped at the library door, straightened his bow tie, and smoothed his hair. "Do I look okay?"

"Um, yes," Stephen said. "Why?"

"Ivan hasn't met Isaac yet," Sofia said. "He wants to make a good impression."

"There are certain kinds of friends a good detective can always use," Ivan said, "and a scholar like Isaac is one of them."

"And like I said, he's cute." Sofia smiled. "Just be yourself with him. He's not like you expect."

"What I expect is beside the point. He is a genius, and given all the things Edmund is—none of them is being dim—it's a good thing he's here." Ivan adjusted his suit coat, then entered the library.

With a shrug to Stephen, Sofia followed.

Ivan paused at the first reading table they came to, next to one of the swirling staircases to the library's upper level. Books didn't have to be plucked off the tall shelves here. No, they *flew* to you after you picked their card from the catalog.

But Ivan made no move toward the catalog drawers. "Excuse me, erm, sir?" Ivan said, addressing the whole room.

Nothing happened.

"Might we have a quick word of consultation?" Ivan tried.

Still nothing.

"Maybe he's not here," Stephen said.

"Isaac!" Sofia called out. "It's Sofia. We met yesterday. You here?"

"Show some respect," Ivan said.

"Present!" A voice floated down from the upper level of bookshelves.

Stephen still didn't see anyone.

"Look harder," Sofia said, apparently sensing his confusion.

A narrow walkway ran along the second level of the library, and sure enough, when he squinted, he made out a tiny head poking up from the railing.

A chubby, bright green worm about the length of a pencil wavered back and forth as he peered down at them. Isaac—a bookworm?—wore a flat, tasseled cap like Stephen had seen at graduation ceremonies, and a pair of glasses, with no earpieces, balanced at the end of his nose.

He was, in fact, cute.

"Hi again, Isaac," Sofia said.

"Learned Isaac of the Istanbul Academy, it is truly an honor to meet you." Ivan lowered his head.

"Sofia," Isaac said with a whine. "Why'd you bring this stuffed shirt here?"

Ivan's head popped up, affronted.

"Ivan is my best friend," Sofia said. "And this is our other best friend, Stephen. We need your help."

The bookworm wriggled in what might have been the bookworm version of a shrug. "Fine, I'll play nice," Isaac said. "Give me a sec."

The little worm made his way down the railing. Despite his small size, he could move fast. So fast that his glasses fell off when he stopped. "I don't suppose one of you could pick those up?"

Stephen plucked the tiny pair of glasses off the floor. "I've never seen glasses without earpieces on them before."

"They're called *pince-nez*," said Isaac. "They don't have earpieces because—"

"Because worms don't have ears—got it," finished Stephen.

"Well, *bookworms* don't have ears," Isaac said. "Earworms do, of course."

"Of course," Stephen said, though he hadn't thought an earworm was an actual worm, just a song that got stuck in your head.

"Now put them back on me." Isaac rolled his little eyes.

Stephen carefully replaced the worm's glasses.

Isaac blinked up at him. "Thank you very much! Now, what can I do for my new pal Sofia?"

Ivan shook his head, but said, "The Sphere of Crystal Vision. What can you tell us about it?"

"Is that what *you* want to know?" Isaac asked Sofia.

"Yes," she said. "And be nice to Ivan."

"It's just I meet a lot of people in suits, and they are *so* boring," Isaac said. He shut his little eyes and made a snoring sound.

Stephen had to swallow a laugh. "Ivan may be many things, but boring isn't one of them."

The worm looked Ivan up and down. "I'll take your word for it." Then his eyes crossed, and rings of yellow light started expanding rapidly outward from the centers of his pupils. "Let me just search my index for your sphere."

When the yellow rings stopped, Isaac said, "The sphere is a device with two main powers. It was made from remnants of crystal balls and scrying mirrors, and like them, allows a viewer with magic to witness events across time and space. If so desired, it also permits travel to the place and time viewed." The bookworm paused. "I don't write this stuff, you understand. It's a little dry for my taste."

"The sphere has a new use now," Stephen said. "Dragon bling."

"I like the sound of that," Isaac said. "Tell me more."

"Shhh," Sofia said. "Ivan's thinking."

Isaac mouthed the words *Ivan's thinking*, making fun. But he did stay quiet.

Ivan tapped his finger against his lips.

Finally Stephen asked, "Ivan, what *are* you thinking?"

Ivan lifted his index finger into the air. "Hypothesis: our nefarious foe used the Sphere of Crystal Vision to spy on Hakor in the Grove of Memory in the past and learn the answer to his riddle."

"The Grove of Memory in Egypt?" Isaac asked. And then the worm made a buzzing sound as if Ivan had gotten the answer wrong on a game show. "I don't know about the rest, but the part about the grove isn't possible. There are some places that are too secret and sacred for scrying devices to work. The Grove of Memory is one of them."

Ivan frowned. "I don't suppose there's a description of the grove in your index either."

"This kid's funny," Isaac said. "Not a chance. Only that it's located in the Hall of Sand and Wind and accessible to sphinxkind alone."

"We're back where we started." Ivan stood. And then he kicked the leg of the table.

Sofia and Stephen raced to his side.

"Whoa, whoa, whoa!" Isaac said. "No one except me assaults library furniture!"

Sofia put her hand on Ivan's arm. "It's okay. We'll figure this out."

"Wait," Stephen said. "What about the second use of the sphere? The travel-to-the-where-it-was-viewed part?"

Ivan blinked at him, and after a long moment, a grin split his face. "You're a genius!"

"Technically I am the only genius here," Isaac said, huffy.

Ivan ignored the bookworm. "He must have spied all the way up to when Hakor went in the grove. He could have gone back and wrangled his way in behind Hakor somehow to get the answer. Bek said we must have proof he entered the grove."

Gone back? Hadn't that other Darkfell guy mentioned something about the clockwork sundial? And hadn't Madame Veronika said it could be used for time travel? "So, he could have used the clockwork sundial to travel to the grove?"

"Yes," Ivan said. "But Edmund wouldn't have used the Darkfells' clockwork sundial because it would have been too easy to trace—too risky. The Octagon told the family they had to stop using it. The Sphere of Crystal Vision has no such rule. As long as he could see when Hakor entered the grove, he'd know the time he needed to go back to." He stroked his chin, thinking again.

Stephen had read enough comic books to know that time travel always had rules. Learning them up front was important. Otherwise you'd end up with split time lines, or fighting villainous versions of yourself. "How does it work? Time travel, I mean."

"Supernormal time travel differs from normal time travel in several important ways," Ivan said.

Stephen held up his hand. "Wait. There's such a thing as *normal* time travel?"

Ivan answered, "Yes, we're all doing it all the time. The only way for normal people to travel through time is forward, at a rate of one second per second."

"Oh," said Stephen. He'd never thought of it that way, but he supposed he *was* moving through time, well, all the time.

"Time travelers can go anywhere and anytime in the past," Sofia said. "With the right object."

"What about the future?" asked Stephen. "Could we use some object to go forward a few days and ask ourselves what we should do? Future us will know more about what's going on than present us, right?"

"Sure," Isaac said sarcastically. "If you're into paradoxes."

Ivan said, "First, time travel can't be used to move forward to times that have not yet been created. Second, time travelers can make no significant changes in the past."

Stephen thought he got it. "But they could witness things in the past and use the information once they return to their own time."

"Thus, Edmund," Ivan said. "Our foe."

Isaac the bookworm let out a whistle. "*You* know Edmund? I had no idea. Now we're talking. Do you think I could get an audience with him? He might be the only person in this town smarter than me."

Ivan, Sofia, and Stephen looked at one another. Even the hard-to-impress bookworm could be whammied.

"We'll see what we can do," Ivan said. "Thank you, Isaac. You've been most helpful."

"Any friend of Edmund's!" the little worm sang out as they left the library.

"What do we do now?" Sofia asked.

"Yeah," Stephen said. "If Edmund did go back in time, what does that mean for us?"

"It means that's where the proof is," Ivan said. "And that the only method we know to get to there and then has become part of Cindermass's horde. Inaccessible to us."

Oh no. "Edmund *is* an evil genius," Stephen said.

"Yes, yes he is." Ivan raked his hand through his hair. "And we're running out of time."

CHAPTER ELEVEN

Stephen headed out on foot to his mother's apartment, glad she was close enough for him to go there safely on his own. Well, he was on his own *now*. Ivan and Sofia had escorted him to the hotel's back exit—Ivan insisted they all needed to keep a low profile to avoid Edmund.

The sidewalks were busy, so Stephen had to thread his way through the people, mostly heading home from work by the tired and harried looks of them. Ivan and Sofia planned to spend the time he was gone trying to come up with a strategy to get the proof they needed. Stealing the sphere from Cindermass's neck was not an option—and even if he *wasn't* under Edmund's thrall, he wouldn't be able to so much as loan it to them.

Although even if he could . . . Would that mean time travel? That felt impossible. Even in his new impossible world.

Stephen let the situation rumble around in his head on the walk to his mother's apartment. Fae usually traveled to Faery using special gateways under open sky, and so, being near Central Park made it easy for her to go there as needed. She even had a fae knight who lived next door and served as a sort of valet and head of security. His name was Sir Quartzmane, and he was another member of the Primrose Court—as was Stephen, though he still didn't really understand what that meant. His mother hadn't asked him to go to Faery yet, and he hadn't offered.

When Stephen reached the building—seven stories tall with a royal purple awning over the entrance—the regular human doorman tipped his hat. "Your mother said to buzz you right up."

The building was as ritzy inside as out, with an old-fashioned mosaic floor, and an elevator the doorman had to allow you to use to get to your

destination. Stephen's mother lived on the top floor; "closest to the sky and farthest from the asphalt" was how she'd described it to Stephen. Apparently there was a rumor that fae people didn't like cities because iron and other metals in such large concentrations bothered them, but she said it was more that they preferred to keep some connection with the natural world. His mother had explained that unlike many fae, who preferred to live in Faery or a forest, she, like most artists, could find nature anywhere. She'd tilted her beautiful blue face at Stephen and asked if he agreed.

He'd nodded. And since then he'd done a much better job of paying attention to the trees and the birds and the bits of grass poking through the sidewalk. She was right. If you looked, nature was everywhere, even in the city. And *especially* in Central Park, which the wide windows of her painting studio overlooked.

He rode the silent elevator up, and was surprised to hear familiar voices when he exited into her hallway. The door to his mom's apartment was open. As he got closer, he saw some members of the Octagon were visiting. Or rather, about to leave. Aminata, the human representative, stood just inside the door with her hand on the knob, but she had turned back to talk to the others.

Madame Veronika and Chenghiz, the giant fire-bird, were there, too. And of course, his mother. They seemed to be in the middle of a conversation that hadn't quite finished yet.

Stephen stopped on the threshold. "Um, hello again," he said uncertainly, and Aminata flinched and grabbed Madame Veronika's arm. "Sorry," he added. "I didn't mean to startle you. If you, um, need to talk, I can wait in the art studio."

His mother glowed at him, smiling in a way that made him feel the simplest version of happy, and then nodded. The stones in her tiara sparkled. "If you don't mind. We'll be but a moment to conclude our business."

But Stephen hesitated, even as Aminata stepped aside to admit him. He glanced between all these supernormally important people and considered the day he'd had with Ivan and Sofia.

"What is it, young man?" Aminata asked, her wrinkled skin creasing with concern as she peered through her half-mooned glasses. "Do you have something to tell us?"

"I'm just curious. None of you believe Edmund's great, right?" Stephen asked.

"No, we don't." Madame Veronika's voice was musical, pitched low.

Her cat accompanied her, Stephen discovered, as Jersey Pete wove through his legs, rubbing against his ankles with a loud purr. "But Edmund's already been using the wand, hasn't he? Why wouldn't he start with you guys first?" Stephen asked. "If he was changing people's minds?"

"The members of the Octagon are protected by magical safeguards," his mother put in. "For obvious reasons."

"But not by infallible safeguards," Chenghiz spoke, and added a sound half like a squawk and half like a lion roar. His feathers glowed the soft red of banked coals.

"No, not infallible ones," his mother said.

"Mrs. Gutierrez is letting him move into the hotel, and everyone else seems to think he's the best," Stephen said. "Except us—me and Ivan and Sofia. Why is that?"

"Ah," Madame Veronika said. "An excellent question. There are safeguards like those that protect us, and then there are natural safeguards. Your youth makes you more difficult to trick."

"As does our fae nature," his mother added.

"Oh." Stephen tried to absorb this. "So, it's not permanent—the people who are affected. You can still stop him from becoming king?"

Madame Veronika raised her eyebrows. "You and your friends certainly know everything that happens in the Hotel New Harmonia, don't you?"

Stephen shrugged. "Ivan's a detective."

Madame Veronika waited a moment, as if deciding to speak. She glanced at his mother, then said, "He has begun a spell that is spreading throughout the supernormal world. It will become permanent with the rise of the crescent moon tomorrow night.

That's the final stage of his taking control. But we will find a way to stop it."

Jersey Pete meowed and left Stephen to return to the side of Madame Veronika's well-worn boots.

"Yes, we will." His mother backed up a step and gestured for Stephen to go through the living room to the studio. "I'll just be one more moment. You try not to be troubled."

He nodded at her, and this time he made it a few steps before he stopped. He gazed up and up into the sharp eyes of Chenghiz. Who gazed right back at him. "What is it, boy?" the giant bird asked.

Stephen squared his shoulders. "I should tell you something else. Cindermass met with Edmund. Edmund gave him a gift and . . . Cindermass thinks they're friends."

Chenghiz's eyes narrowed, and his beak turned a brilliant shade of red as it parted. "I knew that dragon must be involved."

Stephen rushed ahead. "It's the wand. They'd never met before. Cindermass didn't have anything to do with all this until today. We think Edmund must just want you guys to believe that. A distraction."

"'We?'" Aminata asked. "You and your friends again?"

"You must promise me you won't go near Edmund," his mother said.

"We don't plan to," he said, because it was true. "I just don't want anyone to waste time fighting with Cindermass."

"Fair enough," said Aminata. "You are an interesting young man. Of course, with your mother, who could expect differently?"

"Or with my dad," Stephen said, feeling the need to be loyal to him, too.

"Of course," Aminata said.

With that, Stephen figured he was dismissed, and carried his book bag to his mom's studio. Her apartment was all hardwood floors and high ceilings, sparsely furnished so the rooms felt open and airy. The low murmur of voices continued behind him as he made his way into the studio and set down his stuff.

The large rectangular easel with their joint painting on it was out and ready for their work to continue, a fresh palette of paints and two clean brushes set up beside it. The painting was a landscape, a study of the park. They'd been working mainly on capturing tall trees that rustled softly on the canvas as if they moved in a breeze.

The murmuring outside finally stopped, and Stephen heard the click of his mother's footsteps as she made her way across the wooden floor to the studio. He didn't turn around, and she came to a stop at his side.

"I've been noticing trees more out there, in the world," he said. "Since we painted these. Does that sound dumb?" He glanced over.

She studied Stephen instead of the painting. "That's to be expected. Fae animation requires that we understand how something exists—how it's still and how it moves. That's how we capture its essence. Your gift is encouraging you to notice, so it can better serve you."

"Oh," Stephen said. "But . . . I'd never seen

Cindermass or any dragon fly when I drew him." Had he been that close to getting torched after all when he'd made the portrait of the dragon flying around the Empire State Building?

"But you knew him. You'd observed him."

"Not flying, though," Stephen said.

"Our nature when we're in motion remains when we're still. It's the same with other things as well. Do you want to see something—how would you say it—extremely cool?" She grinned.

He smiled back. "What is it?"

His mother picked up a brush and dabbed it in blue paint, then painted right on the wall. Two wings, a thin body. She looked at him.

"A butterfly?" Stephen asked.

"Yes," she said. "A butterfly." And then she set down the brush and extended her hand toward the small painted butterfly on the wall, staring at it. As Stephen watched, it flapped one wing, then another, then . . .

It took flight off the wall! It fluttered around his head on blue wings. Real wings.

"That was the cool part," his mother said with a wink.

"Wow," Stephen said, watching it. "How'd you do that?"

"The greatest skill of fae animation is bringing an object from your work into the real world. It's called detachment. Someday you might be able to do it, too."

"Really?" It was like a superpower. He reached in his pocket and brought out a small piece of charcoal. "Can I try it?"

"Not today," his mother said, and laughed. She picked her brush up and dabbed it in some white paint. "You're still new to this, and it can be dangerous. You take the blue there, mix it into whatever shade you think the sky is. I'll make the clouds. You'll see how it fits together."

"But the sky doesn't move," Stephen said, disappointed, stowing his chalk. There was something so cool about seeing the lines of his own work taking on movement, beginning to live.

"Doesn't it?" she asked as if the answer was obviously yes.

Which, Stephen supposed, it was. "Right. I guess it only *looks* still," he said.

"The sky's very nature is change. Some parts of it quickly; some slowly, over eons. Good."

She motioned for him to start, and so he took up the second brush and layered on some thick sky blue paint, the way she'd taught him. He'd expected to have to continue using his colored pencils or maybe some kind of small student watercolors. But his mother hadn't ever suggested he not use the same tools as she did—and according to Ivan and Sofia, she was considered one of the best fae artists in history.

Stephen spread some blue, watching as his mother made a cloud on the other side. He wasn't sure how they wouldn't end up making a mess with this approach . . . and shouldn't they have done the sky before the trees? But she mixed her paints herself, with a touch of fae magic, and he trusted her.

He did. Already.

"Mom?" he asked.

"Yes, Stephen," she said, continuing to paint.

"You guys really can't do anything to help Hakor?"

"I'm afraid the only thing we can do is focus on helping everyone," she said, smoothing her paint into a rough cloud, shaped like a bird. "Hakor's fate was sealed by his nature. He was a sphinx, and while it is a great tragedy, it is their way."

Stephen stopped his brushstroke. "I think that philosophy stinks. It's not fair."

Startled, his mother put down her brush and turned. "I forget sometimes you grew up among humans."

Stephen set down his paintbrush. Growing up with humans wasn't the problem. "It's right to step up when a terrible thing happens."

She studied him, her eyes deep with wisdom. She seemed to see more about him than he did about himself. Maybe she did. Maybe she understood him.

"And that," she said, "is your nature. It would be far more troubling to me if you didn't want to do more, rules or no rules."

She hesitated, then put a hand on Stephen's shoulder. "I meant what I said before. You mustn't cross paths with this Edmund the Enchanter. No matter what happens, you leave him to us, all right?"

The words were both encouraging and discouraging. He couldn't ask for advice on the time travel stuff without tipping off their investigation. And then he, Ivan, and Sofia would probably end up ordered to stop trying to prove Edmund had cheated. That would just make everything worse.

"Okay," he said, picking up his paintbrush again. "Now about my sky—what if I wanted it to be sunset?"

She held her gaze on him, suspicious, but then smiled one of those happiness-inducing smiles. "Now that is an excellent question, my ambitious son." She clapped her hands together and turned back to the color palette. "We're going to have some fun. Let the troubled nature of reality take care of itself for a little while."

That seemed unlikely, but Stephen resolved to try—until Sir Quartzmane cleared his throat. He'd moved so quietly, they hadn't even heard him come in.

Sir Quartzmane, as always, was decked out in silver armor. Stephen half wondered if he slept in it. It should have made his movements easy to detect, but Sir Quartzmane could move like a ghost. Stephen suspected it was part of his fae knight skills.

"My lady," Sir Quartzmane said, and bowed.

His mother's lips set in a grim line, and she put aside her paintbrush. "What news is so pressing you'd interrupt my time with my son?"

Sir Quartzmane inclined his head. His eyes had deep lines around them. "The La Doyts have asked for a meeting with the Octagon. They think they may have a break on the case."

"Of course. We can take Stephen home on the way." His mother sighed, taking Stephen's paintbrush and placing it and her own into a small clay cup of water. "I'm sorry that our lesson must be cut short today. You understand?"

"Stopping Edmund is more important than anything else right now," he said.

"Yes," his mother said, "but still not more important to me than you are. I know it may be hard to believe since I was away for so long, but it is true. My love for you is in *my* very nature."

"Me, too." Stephen blushed as he gathered his backpack, his heart full. "Here's hoping next week we aren't in the thrall of an evil sorcerer, and can make up the lesson."

CHAPTER TWELVE

After his mom dropped him off at the curb, Stephen walked in to find the hotel lobby quiet. He wasn't so worried now that he knew his age protected him from Edmund's spell, at least for the time being. But he still took a good look around.

A clerk with pale yellow skin was assisting a tall man made of bark at the desk, but otherwise, the lobby was deserted. So he noticed the elevator right away.

The elevator opened and closed with an almost frantic *bing bing* each time its doors split apart, the lights above it flashing in a cycle. Stephen rushed toward it.

"Stephen, finally you're back!" the elevator cried. "Get on before anyone else sees you!"

Enough strange things had happened lately

that this hardly seemed to count as one. Stephen boarded, noting the bark-skinned man headed their way. Tendrils of vines grew from the crown of his head instead of hair. "Hold that—" he said.

But the elevator doors slid shut right as he picked up his step.

"What's wrong, Elevator?" Stephen said.

"Ivan and Sofia asked me to bring you up to the Village straightaway once you got back," the elevator said. "To protect you from this *Edmund*. I encountered him for the first time earlier, and I can understand *why*! He is so smug and conceited; never even said a word of hello to me—talked to Carmen about how beautiful the city is, particularly the park, when he must *know* I'll never see any part of it. Why, he is a villain!"

"Yes, he is." Stephen smiled. At least the elevator wasn't whammied yet. "But I think the La Doyts may be about to figure things out where he's concerned. They called a big meeting."

"I know all about it!" the elevator said. "Well, a little about it. Anyway, the meeting is why I was told to bring you to your friends immediately with no stops."

Sir Quartzmane had said there was a break in the case. But this sure didn't make it sound like the meeting was a good thing. Stephen's stomach dropped.

"I hate that you had to miss out on your evening with your mother," the elevator said. "I for one look forward to the day the Manager lets a painting by the two of you grace the walls of the hotel. Not that he'll let me see it. I'm just an elevator, after all, so what could I possibly know about art?"

"I'll make sure you get to see it if that happens," Stephen promised.

The elevator heaved a sigh and stopped on the Village level, the roof. "Thank you. What would I do without you? Go up and down, miserable as in the old days—yes, I know the answer, but still." The doors slid open. "Be careful."

"I will," Stephen said.

He stepped out to discover the Village was quiet, too, despite it not even being dark out yet. No monkeys or gargoyles in sight. He half expected to see a tumbleweed blow across the green. The silence felt eerie.

Stephen tried to keep his steps calm, but eyes seemed to be watching him. And then he heard it. The whistle.

High and thin, a short melody. It repeated.

He hesitated, then sped up, hurrying toward his cottage.

The whistle came again. He was practically jogging.

And so he nearly jumped out of his skin when Sofia grabbed his arm and towed him toward the gazebo. "Come on," she said. "Why didn't you respond to the signal?"

"What signal?" Stephen asked.

Sitting on the bench inside the gazebo, Ivan had his fingers to his lips and had clearly been the source of the whistle. He lowered them. "It seems we may have forgotten to share the signal with you. Get in here, and quick. We have a serious situation. Or I should say, our serious situation has gone from bad to worse."

"I got that impression from the elevator," Stephen replied. "What is it?"

"The unthinkable happened," Ivan said. His eyes were wide behind his glasses. Stephen hadn't seen him this rattled before.

"He's not exaggerating," Sofia said, sitting down in the shadows of the gazebo.

Ivan nodded. "My parents went to Edmund's suite on twelve to interview him. They were attempting to use the Infallible Suggestion Serum, which was invented by my mother's ancestor the redoubtable Agatha Milion. If it had worked as it should have, he would have been moved to turn over the wand. Instead he ensorcelled my parents. Right this second they're suggesting the Octagon not even try to stop Edmund!"

Ivan's voice had risen as he talked, and Sofia softly shushed him. "Low profile," she said. "Remember?"

"If he managed to get the drop on my parents, Edmund's plan is complex, elegant, and superbly executed. We won't last long if we stick around here." Ivan sobered even more. "We must get access to an item that will allow us to follow Edmund's trail back in time, to find our proof."

"What? How?" Stephen said.

"We need to go to talk to Bek." Ivan looked past Stephen. "Here's our ride now. Since time is of the essence, we sent Bek a note via gargoyle and asked if she could send someone to pick us up."

Ivan strode out to where a—well, Stephen guessed it was another sphinx—landed on the Village green. He and Sofia followed.

This sphinx didn't have human features. Instead he had the curling horns and head of a ram, and a lion's body, but he was bigger than any regular lion. He padded across the rooftop toward them, muscles flowing with the strength and ease of an undammed river, and bowed his giant head. "I am Bek's cousin Amun, here to watch over her until a new mentor is assigned. Climb on."

"Um, climb on what?" Stephen asked, of both Amun and Ivan.

Sofia was already following orders, though. She put one foot over and then held out a hand to Ivan to pull him up. Stephen climbed on behind Ivan, nervous about riding a sphinx. Why were they going to see Bek? What did Ivan mean about getting another object?

But Ivan seemed determined. Maybe he'd thought of a way they could fix everything.

"Hold on tight," Amun said.

Sofia curled her fingers around the downward curves of Amun's horns, alongside his head, while Stephen settled for gripping Ivan and Sofia tightly.

But Amun didn't have wings, Stephen suddenly realized. "How will we . . ."

His voice died as Amun ran at top speed across the rooftop on his big, soft paws and then launched upward, running through the air itself, and they were flying through the night on the back of a wingless sphinx, with the wind in their faces.

It took only a few moments for Amun to run-fly them from the New Harmonia to the New York Public Library, but every one of those moments was *terrifying*. The big sphinx banked and twisted

through the air, careening between the tall buildings and dodging streetlamps.

At one point, Stephen looked over and saw that
one of the famous red-tailed hawks of Manhattan was
flying right beside them. It winked at him and said,
"Hello!" before flapping its wings and darted away.

"Did you see that?" Stephen asked Ivan and Sofia,
shouting over the rush of the wind.

"What?" replied Sofia.

"A hawk just flew by and said hello!"

Ivan said, "Hawks never talk to anyone besides
other hunters."

Stephen was about to protest that this one most
certainly had, but then they were wheeling in to
land in front of poor, petrified Hakor. As before,
the normal people walking down the nighttime
sidewalk didn't seem to see them at all.

Bek crouched miserably beside Hakor's unmoving form. She didn't so much as look up when the
three of them dismounted her cousin.

"I will take my position on Bek's plinth," said the
bigger sphinx. "But soon, she must resume her guard.

We all mourn the passing of Hakor, but the duties of a sphinx must always be carried out, even on the darkest days. So, young Ivan, I hope your news is good."

Ivan said softly, "Would that it were."

"I'm sorry to hear that," Amun said. Then he bounded over onto the empty pedestal and sat back on his haunches. If Stephen squinted just right, he could almost see the stone lion the normal passersby saw.

"Why are we here again?" Stephen asked.

Ivan walked over to Bek.

"It's the only plan we could come up with," Sofia said.

Unease prickled at the back of Stephen's neck. He and Sofia joined Ivan in front of Bek.

"Bek," Ivan said, placing his hand on the girl sphinx's shoulder. "I have to tell you something. Several somethings. And then ask you a serious question."

"Did you figure out how to prove Edmund cheated?" Bek raised her head, a glimmer of hope in her eyes.

"We believe," Ivan said, with great care, "that we

know how Edmund did it. He went back in time to steal the answer to the riddle."

Sofia butted in with a question. "That would be possible, wouldn't it?"

The sphinx tilted her head, perking up. "The Grove of Memory would be very difficult to breach, but if someone did so . . . Yes. They would need to know precisely when the sphinx's riddle was recorded there. I cannot say more." Bek pushed onto her feet, purring. "But this must mean you are close to proving it, then? And Hakor will be back to his old self!"

Ivan pushed his glasses up his nose. "I'm afraid that is why we came. Edmund the Enchanter has done his best to ensure that we have no means to prove he cheated. And he's started a spell to make himself ruler of the supernormal world. Once he completes it, there's a good chance he'll change the rules, so it won't matter."

The hope faded from Bek's eyes.

Ivan didn't look away. "But there may be a way. You're not going to like it."

"I don't care if I like it; I want my mentor alive

and well," Bek said. "You are his friend. I thought you were mine, too. If you are, you'll understand I will do whatever must be done."

"We can't fix this problem from here," Ivan said. "You must allow us into the Cabinet of Wonders. If we can find an object to travel back to the time when Edmund stole the answer, we can get our proof."

Bek studied them each in turn. "I cannot abandon my duties."

"We don't have much time," Stephen said. "When I was at my mom's, Madame Veronika was there. The spell will be permanent after the rise of the crescent moon tomorrow."

Ivan looked at the sidewalk, and his voice was strained when he spoke. "We will try to come up with another way, but . . ."

Bek let out a low growl of frustration. "No. If you go back, you can get proof. That's what you said, correct?"

Ivan nodded.

Bek turned to glance at the library behind her.

"The Cabinet holds the Sundial of Ineb-hedj. It is the least dangerous of the collection's time travel devices."

Sofia shook her head. "But you just said you can't abandon your duties, and the Docent won't allow us to take the sundial or anything else from the collection."

"The Docent will if you will answer my riddle," Bek said.

"But you're an apprentice," Ivan said quietly. "You don't have a riddle yet."

Bek's expression was unreadable. "I do, and you will correctly answer it. Of that I am certain."

"But we can't!" Stephen blurted. If they did what she suggested, she'd be stone, too.

The others seconded him. "No, Bek," Sofia said.

Amun jumped from his seat on Bek's plinth and stalked over. "You can't be serious, cousin."

"You'll be here to guard the Cabinet," she said. "I am serious."

"Oh, little cousin," Amun said, "what can I say to stop you?"

"Nothing," she said. "You would do the same in my position."

Amun hung his head, conceding the point.

Ivan stepped closer to the sphinx girl. "Bek, Hakor would not want it. You'll be stone. We could fail."

Her gaze swept over Sofia and Stephen and settled back on Ivan. "I trust you. I trust all three of you. You go get the proof, and when Hakor is restored to life, he can fix me, too. It's a mentorship power."

Bek leaped, and with a flap of her mighty wings, soared to her plinth. There she sat, solemn, waiting.

Ivan, Sofia, and Stephen exchanged glances and slowly approached. Amun watched.

"Bek, are you absolutely sure this—" Ivan tried.

But she interrupted. "Amun, you keep the time." The same hourglass Bek had used the other day appeared out of thin air, and Amun held it.

"If I must," he said.

Bek nodded. Then to Ivan she said, "You promised me you would do whatever you could. And so here is your riddle:

"I grind down mountains,
cover all in my way.
My only fear is
a sunny day."

It was the riddle Ivan had written in his notebook, the one he'd asked Hakor yesterday. This might not be cheating, but it felt the same to Stephen.

Amun turned the hourglass—not that it mattered.

"We're all agreed?" Ivan asked.

"I'm in if you are," Sofia said as the sand fell.

"Me, too," Stephen said, solemn.

Ivan's hands were trembling. Finally, with a glance at Bek, he nodded. "We can do this. I believe in us. If the proof is there, we'll find it."

"Amun, can you tell our parents where we've gone?" Stephen asked. "And that we'll be back tomorrow night?"

The sphinx inclined his head.

"Then let's do this," Sofia said.

"For Hakor," Stephen added, "and for Bek. And for the Octagon."

"Fools," Amun said, but it was gentle. He held the hourglass higher.

"What is your answer?" Bek asked Ivan as if Amun hadn't spoken.

Ivan took a step forward so he stood directly in front of Bek. "You're a glacier," he said.

No one immediately moved—except for Bek, who reached out one furry leg and touched Ivan's shoulder with a paw. "Be quick," she said.

And she lowered her paw. But they didn't run to the Cabinet of Wonders. They stood and waited as Bek oh so slowly, then all of a sudden, went from being a living, breathing sphinx to a creature of immovable stone.

CHAPTER THIRTEEN

The library was closed at this time of night, but Stephen was hardly surprised to discover that it didn't matter. As they approached, the door opened all by itself.

Or not. Stephen felt the same breeze he'd felt the other day float over them as they entered the quiet, dark library. "The Unseen Guardians?" he asked.

"Yes," Sofia whispered.

The soft wind buffeted them toward the cabinet. The Unseen Guardians wafted ahead and swirled around them as they laid their palms on the door. Then it opened and they walked inside.

The cabinet was exactly as it had been the day before. "No opening or closing hours," Sofia said, apparently guessing Stephen's line of thinking.

The treasures on pedestals and open books and strange objects were all in place. As was the Docent. It waited for them at the end of the hallway, hovering there, blue and purple and wispy and worried.

"You do not *have* to take an item," the Docent said. "You could leave this place."

Ivan still hadn't spoken.

"But then Bek would be stone forever," Stephen said.

"And Hakor, too," Ivan said. "We are doing what we must. Please bring me the Sundial of Ineb-hedj."

The wind gusted around them, but gently. Maybe the Unseen Guardians approved of their plan. The Docent continued to watch them. "I see your decision is made, all three of you. You must be careful," it said. "And do not stay too long in the past."

"We won't," Stephen said. "We have to get back before Edmund finishes his spell."

The Docent moved nearer. "The sundial will take you where you are meant to be." The moment Stephen started to ask how the Docent could know, it said, "All will be clear eventually."

Sofia clasped her hands in front of her and spoke to the Docent. "I don't suppose you could loan me some weapons. We were in such a rush to get here, I forgot to bring my sword."

"That is not within my power, I fear," the Docent said. "But I wish you luck."

Sofia nodded, as if accepting a great gift.

Of course. All they had was the clothes on their backs. For Stephen that meant jeans and a T-shirt, and in his pockets, a small notebook, a piece of charcoal and a pencil, his wallet and phone (no service in ancient times, he was betting). For Sofia, it was a dress, leggings, and her boots. Plus her decaled nails. And of course, for Ivan it meant whatever was stashed in his secret pockets.

"Ivan, you have plenty of useful things secreted in your pockets, right?" Stephen asked.

"A few," he said. "Well, about twenty. The compass, some items collected or invented by my ancestors."

"That's good at least," Stephen said, and Sofia nodded agreement.

"Okay, here we go," Ivan said.

Gentle winds buffeted them as the Unseen Guardians brought a stone circle with hash marks, and a metal triangle sticking up in the center. It landed on the Docent's wispy palms. The Docent adjusted the dial and then said, "Place out your hands, Ivanos."

He reached out his hands, palms flat, and the sundial floated and landed gently on them. He peered at it, then at the Docent through his glasses. "We're ready?"

The Docent nodded.

Ivan looked at Stephen and Sofia, then turned to the Docent again. "How does it work?"

"You must be touching one another," it said, and Stephen and Sofia gingerly and awkwardly rested their hands on Ivan's shoulders. "Then simply turn in a full counterclockwise circle."

"That's it?" Ivan asked, his voice wobbling with nerves that Stephen felt, too.

"That is it," the Docent said.

"Ready?" Ivan asked.

"Wait!" Stephen said. "How do we come back?"

"Hold it while maintaining physical contact with one another and turn in a clockwise circle," it said. "Whatever you do, don't let it out of your possession."

"Are we ready now?" Ivan asked.

"Yes," Sofia said, and Stephen glanced over to see she'd closed her eyes.

"Not really, but let's do it," Stephen said. He kept his eyes open.

They shuffled in a slow circle, and it didn't feel

like anything was happening until the exact step where Ivan completed the full rotation.

There was a noise like thunder in Stephen's ears, and a smoky smell like a fire that had been burning a long time, and a flare of light as bright as a star. He fell upward, and his hair stood on end, and pins and needles prickled over his whole body, even his eyeballs.

Then he *wasn't* falling. The pins and needles disappeared.

They were somewhere else entirely.

The past?

Stephen took in a mirage-like sight in the shimmering distance. A desert road dotted with palms and a couple of traveler caravans lay between where they stood and *pyramids* in the distance. The pyramids didn't look identical—one had steps instead of the smooth sides he expected.

"Wow," Stephen said. "That's a real live pyramid. More than one real live pyramid. Somehow it's more impressive than a skyscraper."

"And *that*," said Ivan, taking Stephen's arm and

turning him to face in the other direction, "is most certainly the city of Memphis, also known as Inebhedj. Circa 2500 B.C. We made it. We're in ancient Egypt."

"It's loud here," said Sofia. "Really loud."

They stood outside tall stone walls painted white and gleaming in the hot sun burning down on them. And Sofia was right: coming from inside the walls was a din—voices calling, the sounds of musical instruments and what might have been wheeled carts moving, and stray animal noises—all combining into the symphony of a city. A different kind of city than Stephen had ever been to.

He turned in a slow circle, taking it all in—or trying to. Assuming the Docent was correct, this was *the past*. Not the recent past either, but thousands of years ago. Before anyone in his family had even been a twinkle of existence. . . . Or was that true? He didn't know how long the fae lived. He'd have to ask. But anyway, he'd *thought* going through the gateway to Transylvania—which had almost killed him—had been an adventure. But this? This was next level.

Some travelers—dark-skinned and wearing long, flowing clothes—were approaching on the road.

"So . . . what do we do now?" Stephen asked. "Where do we start, I mean?"

"First, we turn off our phones to save the batteries in case we need them for anything later," Ivan said, and they all did and stowed them. "Now I guess we figure out how to get into the city."

"Into a city in *ancient Egypt*. The ancient Egypt I've read about on museum plaques and in books," Stephen said.

"Are you feeling okay?" Ivan asked, a crease between his eyebrows.

"I feel like I'm dreaming. Or in a painting."

"Too hot for that," Sofia said.

"Now, about getting inside the city . . ." Ivan said. Stephen forced himself to focus on practical thoughts. "We look kind of conspicuous, don't we?"

"Clothing aside, I'm probably going to be the least conspicuous," Sofia said.

Stephen and Ivan exchanged a look, frowning. "Why's that?"

She lifted her arm, brown in contrast to the pallor of both boys. "Duh. My skin. Speaking of which, Ivan, you'd better wrap something around your head to keep from burning out here. You don't have sunscreen on."

"You have a point," he said, his forehead already beading up with sweat. He looked as though he was roasting in his suit. He whipped out a handkerchief and frowned some more at it. Sofia sighed, taking it and wrapping and knotting it into a makeshift head covering.

"Should I do something like that?" Stephen asked. He touched the points of his fae ears, which stuck out, too—figuratively and literally.

"Let's play it by ear," Ivan said, removing his jacket and folding it over his arm. "No pun intended. We need to find an Octagon safe house. There would have been a public house or tavern or an inn even in these days. The local supernormals may be able to point us in the right direction."

The travelers had gotten close enough to see them, and began calling out. Of course, Stephen couldn't understand a thing they were saying.

"Come on," Ivan said, and Stephen was glad he seemed willing to take charge.

He hustled them along the wall, and soon enough, they came to a wide break in the wall: an entrance, unguarded. The city noise had only increased in volume.

The travelers had sped up and were gaining on them, still calling out. Sofia had taken up a slightly defensive stance. "Ivan, I don't suppose you have something in your pockets that lets us understand what people here are saying?" she asked.

"Afraid not," he said.

"I say we don't stick around to see what they want," Stephen said.

"Agreed. And if things get dicey," Sofia said, "let me take the lead."

CHAPTER FOURTEEN

They didn't even wait for things to deteriorate. Sofia led the charge as they plunged into the controlled chaos beyond the walls.

Even though she didn't have a sword, Stephen felt confident she could defend them. And that she was by far the best of them to assume the role. Half diplomat, half warrior. That was Sofia.

They were surrounded immediately by a market that seemed to sell all sorts of things—spices and vegetables and meat, wild and less wild animals in simple reed or bamboo cages, cloths and dyes. The smell of hot oil over fire. Maybe they could trade money or coins for clothing to blend in better? And for food when they got hungry? But before Stephen could say so, he noticed a stall with symbols painted on a cloth hanging down from a table, along with arrayed amulets and jars and bottles.

He did a double take at the sight of the supernormal haggling with what turned out to be a witch. The witch had flowing white hair with the texture of cotton candy, and heavily lined eyes in contrast to lips painted pale pink. A thick necklace of some fine metal hung around her neck, and she wore a flowing white tunic.

Like Madame Veronika, she just gave off a *witch* vibe—there was a way about both of them that spoke of magic and secrets.

The supernormal she was talking to had a large crocodile-shaped head and a human body draped in the same kind of cloth most of the people around them had on.

"Is that..." Stephen pointed at the crocodile man, but he didn't have the right word. He looked like drawings of gods from Egyptian mythology.

"Of course," Ivan said. "I can't believe I didn't think of this before. This is before the Great Dweomer took place. Supernormals will be fully visible to everyone here."

"Oh," Stephen said. The dweomer was what hid supernormals from regular humans not affiliated with the Octagon or who hadn't had the powder of True Seeing. "Does that mean I should have covered up my ears?"

"Let's hope not," Sofia said. "Because this seems as good a place as any to find a lead on the grove."

She strode up to the stall and waited patiently, not interrupting, while the witch and the crocodile man finished their conversation. The crocodile man turned his long, treacherously toothed visage toward them and spoke what seemed to be two words as he left the stall with a small amulet in his hand. Two incomprehensible words.

"What do you think he said?" Stephen asked Ivan.

Ivan shrugged.

The witch noticed them and smiled. A warm, welcoming smile. Okay, then.

"Um, hello," Sofia said, doing a curtsy that made the woman's smile broaden. "I don't know if you can understand me, but we're looking for someone. Or for information about someone. His name is Edmund Darkfell. Edmund the Enchanter?"

The witch waved for them to come around the table, and what else could they do? They moved into the stall as she directed.

With a satisfied nod, she then started to putter around in reed baskets that held a variety of things, searching through them until she finally removed a small pot of paste. She plunged a narrow stick into it and turned back to mime for them to open their mouths.

She thrust the stick toward Stephen.

"Ivan?" Stephen asked.

"Go with it?" Not that the boy sounded confident. His glasses were fogged up by the humid heat—or maybe his own sweat—and he hadn't wiped them off. "Hope we don't die?"

Comforting as usual, Ivan.

Stephen crossed his fingers in the hope he would not die an immediate and gruesome death, and opened his mouth. The woman touched the paste to his tongue, then removed the stick. He closed his mouth and swallowed.

It tasted like mud. Mud with spices. But spiced mud was still mud. He didn't have to be a chef's kid to know that.

Ivan and Sofia followed suit, and the witch replaced the pot. She stood in front of them and said, "Did it work?"

"Hey, I understood her!" Stephen said. "I mean, you!"

"Yes," Ivan said, "thank you kindly for the translation assistance. What is your name?"

"Hold on, little time travelers," the woman said. "First, tell me why you are here and why you are using Edmund's name. His passage is still a great sorrow to us."

"Um," Stephen said. Weird that she'd be sorrowful about Edmund's passage. Whatever that meant.

Ivan's eyebrows pinched together. "Edmund made it back to our time and has now put the entire supernormal world in grave danger. He has petrified one— No, I must correct myself. He has caused two sphinxes to be petrified. We need to get to the Grove of Memory immediately."

The witch's lips gathered into a thin, displeased line. She examined them, head to toe.

"I don't believe you," she said. "He left us to go on a foolish quest, which we cautioned him against, and never returned. . . . Not to us, not to the future."

At that moment, calls reached Stephen's pointy ears through the din of the city. The same calls that had followed them outside the city. The band of travelers was approaching, winding their way through the market. "I think—" he started.

But Sofia had heard them, too. She scanned the small space, and spotting a walking stick carved of some dark brown material, grabbed it. She leaped onto the table where the witch had been displaying her wares and then down onto the ground in front of it.

Sofia held the stick not like a sword but a staff, in the center, extended in front of her. "What do you want with us?" she demanded, giving the stick a sinister swirl in the air.

The man in the front had a small girl with braided hair—maybe three years younger than they were—with him. "We saw you arrive," he said. "We knew you must be from the future."

The small girl ducked around the man, and Sofia raised the walking stick only to say "Oof!" when the girl threw her arms around her middle.

"What are you doing?" Sofia asked.

"You must be friends of our friend," the little girl said, hugging Sofia tighter. Stephen understood each word perfectly. "Edmund!"

"Yes," the man said, stepping forward. "We suspected you were newly arrived and wanted to greet you. He was a great help to us. He administered a potion that broke a fever for the young one here."

Sofia wore a frown as deep as any Stephen had ever seen on her face.

"Friends with Edmund?" Ivan said. "You were *all* friends with *Edmund*?"

"Yes. You'd better come with me, children," the witch said, voice cool. "And explain what you're doing here and why you're telling such unbelievable tales about our friend."

Should they run? Stephen didn't know what to do. Even Sofia hesitated; the girl was wrapped around her, but the walking stick still in Sofia's hands was at the ready.

To Stephen's surprise, Ivan gave a nod. "It sounds as if that would be a wise course of action. We can clear up the matter."

"We can?" Sofia asked.

"You'd better hope so," the witch said, a little more darkly than Stephen liked. She busied herself packing away her wares—amulets and more pots of clay and bottles filled with who knew what. Once she'd filled a basket, she thrust it at Stephen. "Make yourselves useful," she said, gesturing to two more full baskets. "And I'd like my walking stick back now, girl."

Sofia, cheeks flushed, handed over the stick and picked up a basket. The travelers continued to stand by, watching with confused frowns.

Ivan pushed his glasses up on his nose, then picked up the woven basket he was to carry. He balanced it awkwardly with his thin arms. "The medicine," he said to the man and his daughter, "the healing potion or what-have-you. What was it? Something magical? Did it have a name?"

The man shrugged. "He called it Aceta-Mino-Phen. Worked like magic; don't know if it was."

"Basically aspirin," Ivan said. "Did he charge you?"

"No, he offered it as a gift," the man said.

Huh. Edmund helping people as charity didn't exactly fit his profile.

"This way," the witch said. "I will take you to my home at the Guesthouse of Bastet. She will decide your fate."

Ivan went pale. "You're taking us to see a goddess?"

Sofia put a hand on Ivan's arm. "She said

'guesthouse.' Surely the rules of hospitality will apply."

"They apply to those from *this* time," the witch replied.

"Wait a second," Stephen said, pausing in the stall. He forced himself to look right at the witch. "Why would we go with you? You haven't even told us your name. Who are you?"

"Are you likely to know who I am, enemy of my friend?" she asked. Then she shrugged. "My name is Dadelion."

Dadelion. The original owner of the ivory wand that Edmund had stolen to make himself king.

CHAPTER
FIFTEEN

Ivan's eyes widened and met Stephen's and Sofia's.

"Come along," Dadelion said. She used her walking stick with a practiced ease. With her white hair, it was possible to guess she was older, but not how old.

No one had threatened them—not exactly. But this was a woman who'd created a mind-control wand and palled around with Edmund.

"Should we run?" Stephen asked under his breath.

"You are a stranger here," Dadelion responded without looking back at him. "I wouldn't suggest it."

They marched in silence through the market with its teeming stalls. Various sellers greeted Dadelion with a nod or tossed her fruit from their stacks—she was surrounded by allies, and they were decidedly not. The only people who *didn't* greet her with smiles were a few other magicians selling amulets and the like. Those men frowned, and she smiled at them.

"Magic was common in these times," Ivan said quietly. "I knew that. But I didn't realize it was this common."

"Theirs barely works," Dadelion informed them over her shoulder with a sniff. "Not like mine. Charlatans, mostly."

Soon she wound them to the end of the marketplace, into quieter, still, dusty streets. Water flowed somewhere in the distance.

Probably the Nile River, Stephen thought, shaking his head again with disbelief.

They came to another set of white walls, and Dadelion nodded to the guards with spears at the entrance. Inside they discovered a sprawling compound made of brightly painted stone. It was covered in images, all feline in nature—cats and people with cat heads crept and capered across the walls. These weren't moving illustrations like those

Stephen could do, but they'd been done by skilled hands.

"The Guesthouse of Bastet," Dadelion said. "In case you were wondering, I am under her protection."

They stopped inside a small courtyard. The guest-house proper was made of bricks and stone, painted the same way as the outer walls. "Bastet," Dadelion called, "I've brought three more strays from the future."

Ivan, Sofia, and Stephen stopped in silent accord, not moving forward to follow Dadelion just yet.

A furred woman with a cat's head appeared in the doorway ahead of them. "Truly?" she asked, her cat's eyes narrowing. She wore draped clothing similar to Dadelion's, but dyed a rich golden yellow. Her fur was inky black, pantherlike in pattern. She grinned at them, showing cat's teeth in a triangular face.

"They've come with some disturbing stories about our Edmund," Dadelion said. "I'm not sure what it means. It seemed best to let you decide what we should do with them."

The cat's smile disappeared. The hair on her neck visibly rose. She growled, adding, "Inside."

"Maybe this wasn't such a great idea," Stephen said to his friends.

"Going with Dadelion or coming to the past?" Ivan asked.

"Either," Sofia and Stephen said at the same time.

"We had no choice," Ivan said. "And now we've no choice but to get them on our side."

He carried his basket through the doorway, and Sofia and Stephen did the same. As Stephen passed the threshold, Bastet took a long sniff of him. "You are from the fae lands, where the creators of chaos dwell."

"I'm not, really," Stephen said, swallowing, "I'm from Chicago. Well, New York now."

"Are those not fae lands?" Bastet said, amber cat eyes scrutinizing him.

How did he explain the United States to someone in ancient Egypt? He just shrugged. "Not at all." Ivan had said they needed to get these two on their side. And so he attempted a joke, even though he knew he'd have to explain it. "More like Cubs and Mets territories—those are sports teams where we're from."

"Sport, eh?" She inclined her cat's head regally. "I do like sport, as do all of my kind. And I sense no ill will in you. Enter."

He did as she said.

The interior was dark and much cooler than the outside. Woven rugs lay in a few spots, and there were bricks set into the floor. There were barrels and small tables. Every other surface was covered with variations on what they had in the baskets. A few clay mugs sat here and there, and what looked to be a bar was at one end of the room. More paintings of cats and—to Stephen's surprise—a few that were clearly dogs adorned the walls.

The three of them set down their baskets and stood uncertainly. Dadelion sank onto a stool at one of the tables and regarded them with a dark look.

"Now," Bastet said, perching with uncanny grace on a seat at the same table, "sit and tell me why you've come, and with stories that trouble my dear Dadelion."

Her deep voice carried a command within it. They sat and glanced warily at one another.

Stephen nodded to Ivan. So did Sofia. He should be the one to speak.

"We are here," Ivan said, "because we promised *our* friend, a sphinx, that we would restore her mentor to life. We're here because Edmund came here to get the answer to her mentor's riddle."

There was a moment of silence.

"Edmund came to learn from us," Dadelion said.

"He was my apprentice for several moons, then he . . . went on an ill-advised journey to the sphinx city. We were heartbroken when we learned he'd failed to gain entry there, and that he would not return. Why should we believe these stories? What do you want from us?"

Ivan stared straight at her. "Do you happen to have an ivory wand?"

Dadelion blanched.

Bastet laid a paw across the table, the tips of her claws extended and hovering over Ivan's hands. "What do you know of Dadelion's ivory wand?" she said, a growl in her voice.

Surprisingly Ivan seemed steadier in the face of Bastet's threat. "I know about it because Edmund has it in his possession. I *don't* know how he convinced you he died, but when he was here, he went to the Grove of Memory. He gained the answer to Hakor of the Nile's riddle and then he returned to our time and used it to get the wand. I also know that Hakor is currently stone. I know that the crescent moon will rise over New York City soon enough and that we may be the only hope of stopping Edmund from using the wand's full power. I know that we do not have much time to waste."

Both Bastet and Dadelion leaned forward.

Before either could speak, a pair of kittens scrambled into the room at top speed. A gray one with a white marking on its forehead like half a spear point skidded on the hard-packed earth as it took a corner too fast, scratching up furrows and howling loudly. Behind came a white-and-gray Siamese kitten with big blue eyes and white paws, giving chase.

A dog with a long, weary face trotted into the room. "I'm so sorry," he said. "They did not expect you home so soon, Dadelion. Hush, hush! Scoot, scoot!"

The kittens completely ignored the talking dog, winding their way between Dadelion's feet and keeping up a loud, constant meowing. The dog followed them, turning in circles when they darted underneath him.

One kitten passed close to Stephen, and he leaned

down and swept it up in his arms. It immediately started purring and kneading his chest. "Here you go, um, sir," he said to the dog. Stephen wasn't sure how to address a talking dog in modern New York *or* in ancient Egypt.

"Thank you. And you may call me Makh," said the dog, the name pronounced like *mac* in *macaroni*. He guided the gray kitten down from Stephen's arms and into another room. The second kitten looked after its companion, then followed when Bastet gently pushed it in that direction.

"A dog lives in your house?" Sofia asked Bastet curiously. "So cats and dogs get along fine in this time period?"

Dadelion answered, keeping her voice pitched low. "Makh was taken in by Edmund as his familiar and had nowhere to go when Edmund passed away. We took him in, and he helps around the house. He and Edmund had a deep bond. I see no reason to upset him unless we can determine you speak truth."

Bastet sniffed. "Let us discuss your claims."

"You believe them," Dadelion said with a note of surprise.

"I am not foolish enough to lie to a goddess," Ivan said.

Bastet nodded her pointy chin. "How else would these children know of the ivory wand?"

Dadelion closed her eyes.

"Pain can make people do unimaginable acts," Bastet continued, "and behave in the strangest ways. Edmund told us his home had not been the most welcoming to him. I always thought he was trustworthy, but he *is* a human . . . and an enchanter."

"And I am human and a witch," Dadelion said testily, eyes popping open at last. "Or do you not trust *me* now?"

"Oh, I trust with you my life, as I always have," said Bastet.

"If you believe us," Ivan interrupted, "then we need two things. We must go to the Grove of Memory as quickly as possible. And we need to know if there is any way to counteract the wand's powers."

Dadelion shifted her gaze from Bastet to Ivan. "In this time and place, only the chieftain of all the sphinxes can allow you access to the Grove of Memory. The Black Ram sphinx."

Bastet hissed and arched her back. "Dadelion!" she said. "These are children. They would never survive the tests the Black Ram puts before those who would speak with him."

"How did Edmund get in there, then?" Ivan asked.

"He's no better than us," Sofia agreed.

"As Edmund's familiar, Makh went with him when he attempted to enter the Hall of Sand and Wind. He may be able to shed further light. But Edmund failed the tests required for entry." Dadelion paused. "In the desert, there is no threat in a felled wizard. I suppose the sphinxes would no longer have bothered with him. He must have used some wizardry to sneak in."

"They would just leave someone who didn't pass their tests in the desert?" Stephen asked.

"Now you begin to understand why no one visits

the Hall of Sand and Wind," Bastet said. "The tests you must pass to gain admittance would also likely mean your death. You will not have magic on your side if you fail. And if Edmund cheated him, the Black Ram will not be pleased to discover it."

"What *kind* of tests?" Stephen asked. "Our friend Bek said that getting in would be the hardest part."

"She is correct," Bastet said. Then she called into the other room. "Makh, can you join us?"

There was a protesting chorus of kittenish yowls from beyond the beaded curtain, but then the long-nosed dog came back into the room.

"Makh," Dadelion said, "I do not know a gentler way to say this: we've learned that Edmund did return to the future."

The dog's eyes held a sorrow in them that faded as he gazed at Dadelion. "He is alive?"

"He was seeking entrance to the Grove of Memory in order to steal information. His failure at the tests may have been intentional," Dadelion said. "A plan to get inside without the Black Ram's knowledge."

Makh said, "My foolish master. That is something he would do."

"These tests . . . ," Stephen said. "What are they?"

Makh turned in Stephen's direction.

"Answer the fae boy," Bastet said.

The dog sat down. He was a large animal, and his head was nearly on level with Stephen's. "Any who seek to enter the Hall of Sand and Wind must first pass the Three Unpassable Tests of Strength, Wit, and Skill."

Unpassable didn't sound good, but Stephen figured Sofia was strong, and Ivan was smart. Maybe the skill test would have something to do with art.

"What are the tests like?" Sofia asked.

Makh said, "I cannot tell you anything more. Part of the rules we agreed to when we entered the sphinx lands. My tongue would not allow it."

"Like with the riddle," Ivan said. "What Bek said that day. Sphinx magic meant no one could repeat the riddle, even if Edmund didn't answer correctly."

Bastet knocked on the table. "Even without details, I hope you understand. It is not such a simple task to go to the Grove of Memory."

"We aren't going home without our proof of Edmund's cheating," Ivan said. "We have no choice but to face these tests and emerge victorious."

Makh turned his baleful eyes on Dadelion and then Bastet. "You would send these three children to their deaths?"

"Let us first debate the dangers and the merits," Bastet said.

CHAPTER
SIXTEEN

The discussion raged for what felt like an hour. Ivan, Sofia, and Dadelion were keen for the three time travelers to set off to the Hall of Sand and Wind and face the Black Ram right away, though their motivations were different.

Sofia and Ivan wanted to finish the mission, confident in their chances. But Dadelion, Stephen suspected, had a deeper motivation she wasn't quite expressing. On the other side, the goddess Bastet had taken up Makh's argument against the notion of any test taking—that it was too dangerous.

Stephen sat off to the side with Makh. The dog lay down so he didn't loom over Stephen; out of politeness, Stephen guessed.

"Are they always like this?" Stephen whispered.

"Dadelion and Bastet? No, no. Well, yes. They are both highly intelligent and passionate individuals, and on those occasions where they do not see facts in the same light, then they argue. With gusto."

"This isn't about facts, though, is it?" Stephen replied. "It's a choice. Whether or not we should go see the Black Ram sphinx and take his tests."

Makh's face was just as expressive as any human's, and it wasn't hard for Stephen to tell that right now, the dog was sad. "They are each hoping some other way will reveal itself, if they argue long enough. But we are strong believers in fate and in signs. You three young people have shown up here with news and a purpose. She may have doubted you at first, but Dadelion would not have brought you here, to the place of her hearthstone, if she did not believe you were fated to do something very important while you are here."

"Well, I *do* think it's pretty important that we not let Edmund take over the world," Stephen said.

Makh didn't quite have the shoulders to shrug.

"I wish he had told me what he was doing. I might have talked him out of it. There is good within him. He rescued me, a magical dog without a family." The dog sighed. "Worse men have ruled the world. At least in our time."

Stephen thought about that for a minute. "Well, that's not really the point. In the future, all the normal countries have rulers, and some of them are good, and some of them are bad, and most of them are somewhere in between. And the supernormal world has the Octagon. But Edmund isn't trying to join the Octagon or run for president, and he isn't giving anybody any choice. Not just a choice of whether or not to vote for him, but a choice of whether or not to *like* him. Sure, he did a spell when he was young that screwed up things for him. But now he's doing the same thing. *Making* people accept him without earning it, whether they want to or not. And that just doesn't seem right."

Stephen broke off speaking when he realized that everybody in the room was looking at him.

"You are right," said Makh. "Bastet, you know

he is. It is time to let them go."

Somehow it didn't sound like an enthusiastic endorsement.

"We promised Bek," Sofia said softly to the cat-headed goddess. "*We* have to think about Bek and Hakor."

Ivan focused on Dadelion. "Can't you give us the wand? I know it would alter the course of fate, but it would also mean Edmund couldn't retrieve it from the Cabinet of Wonders in our time, and none of this would happen."

"That would almost certainly create a paradox," Sofia said, but Ivan kept his gaze steady on Dadelion. "It would be changing something that has already happened."

Dadelion wrung her hands as her face collapsed in anguish. "Would that I could, children. Would that I could. It would be worth the risk."

"You couldn't know," Bastet spoke.

"You did what was right at the time," Makh added.

Dadelion swayed on her feet. "I never should

have created that instrument. To alter someone's mind—heart, emotions, and thoughts—is wrong on the deepest possible level. It is my fault this is happening, and I can do nothing to make it right."

"What happened? Where is the wand?" Ivan asked.

Stephen moved over to stand beside him, and so did Sofia. They made a half moon around the cloud-haired witch.

"A confession was needed," Dadelion asked. "The Black Ram sent for me. I wanted to show everyone how powerful I was. I wanted to help bring justice to the sphinx people. So I created the wand, and when the crescent moon rose, I used it to enspell Kindlefleur. I made Kindlefleur eager to confess, eager to face her exile."

"You were younger then," Bastet said. "We all do the wrong thing at times."

"We all do make mistakes," Stephen said. "But if we own up to them, I think maybe that is all we can do."

"You are young to be so wise," Bastet said.

"I cannot give you the wand, because I do not have it." Dadelion lifted her hands, helpless. "It called to me. The power in it, after I used it. I knew I had done a great wrong. And so Bastet and I did a spell and cast it into the sea; it is forever hidden from both of us. It pains me greatly to learn that it was recovered. That I did not destroy it when I had the chance, and now your future—your world—is in peril. Destroying it would be the only way to stop its power."

Bastet moved to her side and put her arm around the woman's shoulders. "I see that our young travelers must complete their journey."

The dog Makh growled, head shaking from side to side. He quieted and then said, "I will go with you."

Bastet and Dadelion looked at each other, dismayed. "Makh," Bastet said, "don't be foolish."

"I am foolish, perhaps, but also loyal. I will go with them. I can guide them to the territory, and I may be able to help them once we are there."

"I ask only that you children be as kind as you

can to Edmund." Dadelion held up a hand to silence their protest. "I know he is doing wrong in your time, but as Bastet said—pain can make people behave in the strangest ways."

Stephen thought about what Makh had said about there being good within Edmund. If that was true . . . Maybe pain could make people act against their very natures.

"We will do as much as we can to honor your wish," Ivan said solemnly. "How far is the Hall of Sand and Wind? Will we need to find transport?"

"Are there any weapons you can loan me?" Sofia asked, scanning the room.

Dadelion smiled at her. "I do have a gift for you. Take my walking stick," she said. "I'll get another. You will know how to make use of it, if need be. A good witch's walking stick can be almost anything in a pinch—even a weapon."

Bastet rose and buried one hand in Makh's ruff. "You are a brave, loyal fool," she said. "I send with you my blessing."

"Love you, too," he said.

"*Dogs,*" Bastet said, with long-suffering affection.

"Come closer," Dadelion said, beckoning the three children to her.

Sofia carried the walking stick carefully, and she, Stephen, and Ivan did as they were told.

"To get to the lands of the sphinxes, follow this," Dadelion said.

She reached up and removed her necklace of looping, hammered metal and threw it on the floor.

As they watched, it hit the ground not as metal, but as a snake.

"That's a cobra!" Stephen said. Sofia grabbed his arm when he would've backed away.

The snake shimmied in the air, rising up on its body with its great hood flung open. Its tongue flicked out as it regarded them, and then it dropped down to the floor again.

It began to wind in a sinuous rhythm, impossible to look away from. Mesmerizing. Then wind and sand buffeted around them as they traveled—by magic—in a winding path from there to elsewhere.

Sand still flew around them when they stopped moving, and the snake disappeared. They were under a sky like an explosion of colors. Red and yellow and purple and deep blue. A sky that felt big enough to swallow the world, poised over the rolling sand dunes. Stephen's mother had been right: sunsets *were* alive.

On its heels, another thought pushed in: Would he and his mother ever finish their painting?

He scanned the horizon beneath the intense sky.
Ahead in the distance, looming like a warning, was
the stone sphinx he was familiar with from books—
but its face was perfectly intact in this time. Beyond
it were more pyramids. There was a small campsite
in front of them. The sound of the wind swirled in
Stephen's ears.

He looked around then, because none of his traveling companions had spoken. Ivan was sitting in
the sand, and Stephen wondered how much of it
would get in all his many pockets. Stephen's dad
had taken him to vacation at the beach a few times.
Sand was wily. It invaded.

Sofia stood, the walking stick raised in front of
her, as if to ward off attackers. But there were none.

And Makh . . . Makh stared into the distance,
ignoring the spectacular sunset altogether.

"We must go there," Makh said, breaking the
silence. "Where Khafre sits."

"Okay," Ivan said, his voice small in the huge
open space of the desert plain.

Stephen offered him a hand, pulling him up.

"We're going to make it through this," Stephen said. He hoped it was true.

Sofia said, "If we don't, our parents will kill us."

None of them laughed at the joke.

Ivan's shoulders were set, and his face was determined. They began to walk, their feet sinking into the desert sand with each step. Within moments, Stephen's legs were screaming, and it barely felt like they'd gotten any closer.

The wind kicked up again. The sands whirled.

But not viciously—it was almost as if the wind kept the sand from hitting them. "It's the Unseen Guardians!" Stephen shouted.

From the flying sand emerged an almost familiar figure. A torso fading into filmy shadows, a face recognizable as the Docent's.

"I have come to warn you: You have not yet crossed the border of the lands that belong to the sphinx and are home to the Hall of Sand and Wind. But with your next steps, you will cross. It will be too late to go back," it said.

"Did you come from the future?" Stephen asked.

"I am here only to issue a warning," the figure said.

"Look closer," Sofia said softly. "Look how much younger the Docent is."

It was true. The Docent's face was unlined.

The Docent seemed taken aback. "We are to meet again?"

"Yes," Ivan said. "We appreciate the warning, but we have no choice but to enter."

The Docent—who was not the Docent yet—but a guardian of this place, maybe, nodded to them. "You, dog, should not return to this place."

"I'm aware of that," Makh said. "Nothing to be done about it."

The sands swirled again into a giant funnel and then collapsed. The Docent disappeared.

Ivan took a step forward.

There would be no turning back.

CHAPTER
SEVENTEEN

Even at the widest beach Stephen had ever been to, the discomfort of crossing hot sand eventually gave way to the coolness of ocean water. Not here, though. Stephen didn't know which, if any, of the buildings arrayed around the giant stone sphinx was the Hall of Sand and Wind, but he longed for any shade that would give relief from the heat seeping up through the soles of his sneakers.

At least soon it will be dark, Stephen thought. That will cool things down, won't it?

"Makh, I know about sphinx magic, secrets, and all that . . . but is there *anything* more you can tell us about what to expect?" Stephen asked, in part to distract himself.

"Yes," Ivan said. "The smallest thing might come in handy."

"I doubt it." Makh made a dog-sigh. "The tests are extremely difficult challenges constructed by the Black Ram sphinx. He alone conducts and assigns them, and they are designed to exploit weakness in the takers."

"It sounds hopeless," Stephen said.

"Nothing is hopeless," Makh responded.

Sofia bent to scratch Makh's head. "Thank you," she said. "We are lucky to have such a brave guide at our side."

Makh leaned into Sofia's fingers, and she scruffed his fur again before they started to trudge forward once more.

They were much closer to the looming sphinx and pyramids now. Stephen noticed as they approached that the campsite they'd spotted was obviously abandoned—or its inhabitants were hidden somehow.

"What do we do now?" Stephen asked Makh. "Where do we find the Black Ram sphinx?"

The dog had begun panting heavily and did not

answer. He whined, dropped his tail between his legs, and put his snout down behind his two front paws.

"You do whatever I tell you, fae so far from home," an unfamiliar voice said. "And the Black Ram sphinx is already *here*."

There was no way the large creature now standing right next to them could have approached without being spotted, no matter how stealthy it might be. The figure was as big as a horse, with a lion's body, widespread bat wings, a tail like a dragon's, and yes, the head of a black ram, complete with curving horns.

Stephen figured there was no reason to beat around the bush. "We've come to visit the Grove of Memory," he said. "We understand that we have to take some tests first."

The Black Ram said, "You have magic on your tongue, boy. And those clothes you wear are not of familiar make. Who are you? Where did you come from? I know this cur here of old, as the companion of another who spoke boldly of my tests, but you three are no children of the desert."

The Sphinx's Secret

Sofia came to the rescue. "We are from an island on the shore of a land so far from here you would have to cross two seas to reach it. We are all scions of knights. Our parents are in service to the Octagon."

The Black Ram snorted. "I know of the Octagon and its efforts, of course. We participate when necessary. But they have no knightly orders in their service that I have heard of."

"Oh! That's right!" Ivan said brightly. "The Knights of the Octagon won't be founded for thousands of years yet. And the Octagon isn't as powerful now as it will be in the future."

"Bah," said the sphinx. "Time travelers. *Someone* has ensorcelled you with a language spell. But such tricks will be of little use to you as you take the Test of Strength, the Test of Wit, and the Test of Skill."

Stephen swallowed, his throat sand dry. But this is what they had come for. "How are they going to work, exactly? We're ready to be tested, but—"

"They work as they always have. By my will!" The Black Ram sphinx cut him off. "And you may not speak of them, should you ever leave this place . . . which is unlikely."

They stared up at the Black Ram.

He bared his teeth. "The Test of Strength begins now! You, red-haired boy, follow me!"

Ivan blinked and looked from the sphinx to his two friends, then to Makh. "Wait, no. There's been a mistake. Sofia will take the Test of Strength."

"*You* will take the Test of Strength!" roared the sphinx, rearing back up on his hind legs and beating his wings so fiercely that miniature funnel clouds of sand spun crazily in every direction. "And you will fail!"

Ivan must have been trembling. But he hid it as he stepped forward.

At some wordless command from the Black Ram sphinx, a group of human servants walked out from one of the buildings. Two of them unfurled a rug onto the sand while others hung a linen awning above it. One took up position in front of the rug, holding an hourglass bigger than the library sphinxes had used during their riddles. Finally the servants lit torches that illuminated the evening more than Stephen would have thought possible.

The humans silently indicated that Sofia and Stephen should take seats on the rug, and poured water into clay cups from an elaborate container shaped like a hippopotamus.

"We shouldn't be just sitting here," said Sofia, patting Makh when he settled beside her. "And it should be me out there, not Ivan."

"He'll be fine," Stephen told her, trying to sound reassuring. For all their sakes, it better be true.

"Out there" was a large area of desert about the size and shape of a football field. It was marked off by flags set into the sand just outside the two large dunes at either end.

Right in the center, roughly where the fifty-yard line would be, Ivan stood blinking up at the Black Ram sphinx. Even though they were some ways off, Stephen and Sofia could clearly hear their conversation. Whether this was another magical effect or simply the way sound traveled in the desert, Stephen couldn't say.

"You and your companions have elected, of your own free will, to test yourselves against what I will now set before you, yes?" the Black Ram asked. "And all of you accept the consequences for your inevitable failure? You are willing to forfeit your lives?"

Ivan looked over at them, shading his eyes with one hand. Sofia called, "Yes, but we will pass!"

Stephen gave Ivan a thumbs-up, hoping it would make his friend feel better.

Ivan drew himself up to his full height, which was unfortunately not all that impressive next to the oversize supernormal creature. But he spoke clearly and steadily. "I am Ivanos Mercutio La Doyt. We need valuable information you hold that can help two of your own people. If taking these tests is the only way into the Grove of Memory then, yes, we are taking these tests of our own free will."

"Your motivations do not interest me, human child," said the sphinx; rather dismissively, Stephen thought. "Now, behold the Test of Strength!"

The Black Ram sphinx extended a wickedly sharp

claw toward one of the dunes. It was now topped by a large block that hadn't been there before.

In fact, blocks and bricks of various sizes, wooden beams and poles, and other materials were scattered throughout the entire testing area.

"Do you know what a piece of rock such as that might be used for, boy?" the sphinx asked Ivan.

Ivan was sweating, and his glasses had slid down to the very point of his nose. He pushed them up.

"It appears to be one of the large blocks used in the monumental construction projects of this time," Ivan said. "Quarried nearby and moved to the building sites by any one of a number of means still debated by modern scholars."

"No more future talk," said the Black Ram. "Here is your test." The sphinx whirled and pointed at the other end of the field. "There is another dune. In order for you to pass the Test of Strength, the block must rest upon the top of the second dune within one hourglass's time. Starting *now!*"

With that, the sphinx leaped into the air and, flapping its wings extravagantly, flew over to land by the awning shading Stephen, Sofia, and Makh. One of the human servants turned the hourglass over.

"Your time begins!" the Black Ram called.

Ivan protested loudly, "But those blocks weighed an average of two tons each! I weigh sixty-five pounds!"

The sphinx ignored Ivan, instead stalking over to Stephen and Sofia and stretching out so that his great head was under the awning. "With his failure, the other tests will be unnecessary. You will all pay the price."

Makh whined softly.

"This isn't a fair test!" Sofia said, springing to her feet. "Nobody could move one of those blocks by themselves!"

The sphinx chuckled. "I could," he said.

Out in the field, Ivan ran toward the dune topped by the enormous block. He was talking to himself desperately, but Stephen could no longer hear what he was saying. Ivan struggled up the dune, moved to the opposite side of the block, then threw himself at it for all he was worth.

His glasses went spinning into the sand. The block didn't move at all.

Ignoring his glasses, Ivan took a few steps back and raced at the block again. He slammed into the surface and then collapsed against it. His shoulders were shaking.

Stephen had never felt as sorry for Ivan as he did right then. Tears gleamed in Sofia's eyes as she watched.

"Don't count him out," Stephen said. He shared her concern, though.

Out on the dune, Ivan had climbed to his feet. He searched around for his glasses for a few moments, and when he found them, he set them firmly back in place. Then he called across the field. "I can use anything within the flags?" he asked.

The Black Ram sphinx shrugged. "The only rule is that to win, the block must rest atop the other dune before time is up."

Stephen checked the hourglass. The sand was swiftly running from the top to the bottom.

Ivan trotted down from the dune to one of the piles of construction materials. He chose a round pole twice as long as he was tall and, pulling for all he was worth, dragged it up the dune and laid it in front of the block. He did this two more times, setting the poles on the ground parallel to one another.

"What's he doing?" asked Stephen, sitting up.

"He's *thinking*," said Sofia, with a hint of excitement in her voice. "He's making a *contraption*."

"It will make no difference," said the sphinx.

Next Ivan found a pole not quite as long as the others—this one more of a beam, as it was squared off instead of round. He set this on the opposite side of the block, right up against where it rested on the sand. Finally, he went back for one last pole, this one shorter still, but broad.

"Archimedes said," Ivan shouted, "'Give me a lever and where to stand, and I shall move the world'!"

"Oh!" said Stephen. "He's going to move the block over onto those round poles so that they can act as rollers. He'll have leverage. But will it be quick enough?"

"No," said the Black Ram. The amusement in his voice wasn't friendly. "Watch," he said.

Ivan inserted his lever under the lip of the block and angled it back over the square pole, which would act as a fulcrum. He reached up, took the lever by both hands, and heaved for all he was worth.

Stephen was excited to see Ivan slowly lowering himself down to the ground. The square beam had almost disappeared in moving sand. And that's when Stephen realized, simultaneously with Ivan, what was actually happening.

"The block's not moving," said Stephen. "He's just forcing the fulcrum down into the sand."

"Leverage multiplies strength," said the Black Ram. "I do not know who this Archimedes is, but that is known to us. However, it requires something firm to apply the leverage *against*, and a sand dune is not firm."

Out on the field, Ivan kicked the two-ton block, and of course, it didn't move. He slumped down to the ground, with his back to the stone, and put his hands in his pockets.

"Your time has almost expired, Ivanos Mercutio La Doyt!" shouted the Black Ram. "It is permissible for you to forfeit now. Even I could not move the stone from one dune to another in the few minutes remaining!"

At that, Ivan perked up. He looked over at the awning. He shouted, "That's not the test!" Then he darted around to the other side of the block and started digging for all he was worth.

Suddenly Makh the dog sat up.

"What does he mean?" asked Stephen.

"The only rule of the test is that to succeed, the block must rest atop the second dune when time expires," said Makh. "Our host said nothing about moving the block. He might pass yet."

"Unlikely!" came the Black Ram's reply. But he subsided into quiet, too, and they all watched Ivan's next effort with close attention.

Out on the field, Ivan had dug out a small ditch in front of the block. He stacked the three round poles in this, then ran down to the bottom of the dune, almost stumbling.

He turned to face the block, digging in his pockets for a few precious seconds, before producing a stoppered glass bottle.

"Oh, bless the sleuth tailors!" Sofia said.

"Three gusts of the west wind," Ivan said, calling out so they all heard. He held the bottle high. "Captured in 1959 by my great-aunt Cordelia on the Nebraska prairie."

He opened the bottle and pointed it at the dune.

At first, nothing seemed to be happening. But then the true strength of Ivan La Doyt was revealed.

A wind blew from the bottle, and blew the sand of the dune away. From the awning, the dune seemed to move like a wave, sand leaving the playing field altogether. The enormous block sank down to the level of the field, angled up slightly on the three poles Ivan had stacked beneath it.

Ivan ran the length of the field as fast as he could. He circled the second dune, still in its original place—and held up the bottle of wind behind it. As it began to blow, Ivan trotted along behind, using the bottled wind to direct the sand, all the way over to where it resettled under the great block. In just a few minutes, the block was again perched atop a dune.

The sand of the *second* dune.

Ivan had done it.

CHAPTER EIGHTEEN

Ivan waited, his hands clasped in front of his chest, eager for a verdict.

Beside Stephen, the Black Ram grunted in surprise . . . and perhaps he was even impressed. Not that Stephen would've bet money on it.

The Black Ram opened his mouth, baring his big solid teeth, and said, "So you have passed the Test of Strength."

Ivan jumped up with his hands in the air over his head and whooped—and promptly fell over into the sand dune when he landed. Sofia and Stephen ran from under the awning toward him, laughing, but a sudden wind pushed them back. Stephen fought it for a breath, then let it drive him back toward the shelter. Ivan may have passed the Test of Strength, but Stephen would need *his* strength later, too. He was sure of it.

"There will be no celebration," the Black Ram said. "No joyous congratulatory dancing. Two more nigh impossible tests remain."

Ivan made his way to his feet and jogged back over to them. Sand covered him from his glasses rims to his leather shoes.

"Good job, Ivan," Sofia said with a defiant tilt of her head toward the Black Ram.

"Way to go." Stephen held up his hand for a high five, and his palm connected with Ivan's.

Take that, mean old ram sphinx, Stephen thought.

Makh said, "Well done, my boy."

"Enough. I hope you are prepared for the Test of Wit, which will certainly be beyond you, *girl*," the Black Ram declared.

Sofia's eyes narrowed. "We'll see. Where we're from, *girl* is no insult. And it shouldn't be to you either—after all, Bek is training for the same post held by Hakor."

The Black Ram's horned face moved back,

surprised. "You know Hakor? Recently sent to guard the two-headed dragon Tong's treasure house in the Impassible Reaches of Mongolia?"

"He's why we're here," Ivan said, glancing up from polishing his glasses clean of sand with the inside of his shirt. "Though he guards something else in our time."

"No matter to me," said the Black Ram. "We will speak no further of your reasons for troubling me and mine until you have passed the tests."

But if Stephen wasn't mistaken, there was an ever so slight softening in the Ram's regard.

Until he bellowed, "Bring forth the rope!"

The human servants emerged again, seemingly out of nowhere, and this time they carried a long, thick length of rough rope.

"And now, prepare the enchanted knot of Isis," the Black Ram ordered.

The people began to chant over the length of rope each of them held. How could a Test of Wit involve ropes and knots?

Then again, Stephen supposed tying and untying

knots *was* a kind of mental puzzle. One he hoped Sofia knew how to solve.

She was frowning. She'd tucked Dadelion's walking stick under the belt of her dress as if it was her fencing sword back home, and she had her hands on her hips just above it.

"You can do this," Ivan said. "It won't be like the jumbies."

Sofia gave him a look. She reached back to tighten her ponytail, nodded to both boys, and stepped forward.

"What happened with the jumbies?" Stephen asked, low. "And what are jumbies?"

"Little Caribbean tricksters," Ivan said. "Marina has several in her family, and they came to visit once. The jumbies were easily distracted, and Sofia didn't want us to have to entertain them. So she left out a rope with a bunch of knots in it. They wouldn't sleep until the knots were solved, and they were hard knots. She got in big trouble with her mom—who made her spend the next three days untying them herself."

"Huh," Stephen said. "But that means she's good with knots, right?"

"It took her three days," Ivan said. "Patience isn't Sofia's strong suit."

Some of the servants held up a large cloth, and the others ceased their chanting. The people's heads were still visible above the cloth, and they appeared to be moving around one another.

When they stopped, the cloth dropped to reveal a giant, complex knot on the sand. The humans backed away.

The Black Ram said to Sofia, "You, too, will have the length of the hourglass, and your task is to undo the knot in the allotted time."

One of the men turned the hourglass, and sand began to rush through it once more.

Sofia looked at the Black Ram. She looked at the rope. She looked at her hands.

Her hands were nowhere near as wide as the rope was.

"Okay," Stephen heard her mutter. "Okay."

"It will not be okay," the Black Ram scoffed.

"But it *is* possible somehow? This task?" Sofia asked, squinting at the knot, then up at him. "Because otherwise your test wouldn't be fair."

The Black Ram threw his head back in a silent laugh before shaking his head. "Sphinxes are nothing if not fair. Your failure will be yours alone. Now, your time has begun."

Sofia stalked toward the knot on the sand. She poked it with her boot toes. She grabbed the widest strand of the knot with both hands and pulled and pulled, groaning with the effort. Stephen knew how strong Sofia was, and the rope didn't budge.

Because this was a test of wits. Ivan must've been remembering the same thing. *"Think, Sofia,"* the other boy said under his breath.

"And be quick about it," Makh added.

The Black Ram said nothing.

The walking stick tucked under Sofia's belt struck her leg, and she almost tripped.

"Argh!" she said.

Circling the knot, she considered it from every angle. She paused on the far side and turned, smiling, to the people who had prepared it. "Hello," she said, with a sweeping bow. "I'm Sofia Gutierrez from the future, where my parents work for the Octagon. I don't suppose you could be so kind as to help me out with this. The courtesy shown to travelers is important to my family."

It was her best diplomacy. Stephen held his breath.

"There is no help," the Black Ram. "You must do this by yourself. You must use your wits and only that which is on your person."

"I heard you the first time," Sofia grumbled.

One of the women nodded at Sofia as if she was sorry she couldn't do more.

Sofia turned to Ivan and Stephen, and Stephen could tell she was at a loss. Stephen wouldn't have known what to do either.

With a shrug, she circled around the knot again, and this time she *did* trip when the walking stick hit her leg. Sofia, the graceful girl who could vault from a tree without the smallest fumble, fell into the sand, catching herself awkwardly on her hands.

She pivoted on the ground—more like herself—and scowled at the stick. She reached down for it and . . . Yes, it was almost like it *jumped* toward her hand.

"Did you . . . ," Stephen started to ask if Ivan had seen it.

Ivan nodded. "I did. Come on, Sofia."

"Dadelion, you sly sort," Makh said, his voice suffused with love.

Sofia spun the walking stick in her hands and turned back to face them once more. She took a few steps in their direction.

Stephen began to hope.

"I have a riddle for you. How is a walking stick like a sword?" Sofia asked, stalking closer to where the Black Ram waited beside them.

The Black Ram snorted. "You're wasting time. Back to the test."

"I hope this works," Sofia said to Stephen and Ivan.

Stephen reached over, and he and Ivan clasped hands. "What does she mean?" Stephen asked.

Sofia went on. "Dadelion said a good walking stick can be anything in a pinch. . . ."

She whirled on her feet, raced at the knot, bringing the walking stick out in front of her like a sword and slicing down with it—

The rope fell into two halves on the sand.

The walking stick *was* a sword.

Sofia traced a figure eight in the air with her new blade. "I did it, with what was on my person," she said before the Black Ram could protest, if he was so inclined.

"So you did," he said. "It is no matter. You have passed the Test of Strength, and now the Test of Wit. But you will all still face the same fate when the faeling fails the Test of Skill."

"How did you know the walking stick would do that?" Stephen asked, awed, as she approached.

"I didn't," Sofia said. "But I figured there must be a reason it kept getting in my way, and Dadelion said I'd know how to use it, and it could be almost anything. It was like it whispered, *Use me.* So, I thought about what I needed—a sword—and then it was one."

"It's your sword now," Makh said. "It'll be a good, loyal one."

"You must name it," Ivan said.

"Yeah!" Stephen agreed. "Like Excalibur, Sting, Backbiter! But no pressure. It should be something special to you. You can keep it with you even when you're captain of the Perilous Guard."

Ivan cast Stephen a look over his glasses. Stephen knew that Ivan believed the Octagon's rules would somehow prevent Sofia from ever holding the post. A woman had apparently never been captain of the guard. But it was Sofia's dream.

And naming the sword might stretch out the time between this moment of victory and his own test. He was not at all sure he'd pass the way his friends had.

He didn't want to let them down.

Sofia stared down at the sword. It had hieroglyphs on the hilt, and a fine thick blade that looked exceedingly sharp.

"I'll name it 'Mother,'" she said. "Because I'll use it to be one of the greatest protectors the Octagon has ever known." She grinned. "And Mom will say she hates it but secretly love it."

Clever. Mother wasn't any stranger a name for a sword than any other word, Stephen supposed.

"Do you think I don't know you're delaying?" the Black Ram said. "I sense your fear, fae boy."

"Half fae," Stephen said, his heart beating like a drum. "And I don't think you need extra senses to know I'm scared right now. So . . . what is it? What's my test?"

The Black Ram smiled.

CHAPTER NINETEEN

"**The** final test is the Test of Skill," said the Black Ram sphinx. "And it is the simplest of all. You must enter the Hall of Sand and Wind."

That does *sound simple*, Stephen thought. *Which almost certainly means it's anything* but.

"Which one of these buildings is the hall?" he asked the sphinx.

The Black Ram skimmed the nearby structures with a casual glance. "These? No, none of *these* are the Hall of Sand and Wind. These are all human structures, conceived in the minds of women and men and built by their hands. The Hall of Sand and Wind is *there*!"

The sphinx trained his gaze upward, and just then a shadow fell across the desert. An enormous kitelike structure floated slowly across the sky, a billowing contraption of silk and canvas fluttering from a confusing crosshatch of wooden beams. It was lit from within, plainly visible in the evening sky. The walls rippled in the wind, cloth dyed in the colors of the desert sunset they'd seen earlier.

Sphinxes of every description perched like gargoyles on the eaves, or flew through the sky around the floating city.

As they watched, one whole side lowered like a reverse window shade, revealing a cavernous interior lit with thousands of oil lamps. Horns sounded, and every sphinx in sight except the Black Ram flew into the hall as swift as arrows.

"The horns mark the beginning of your test. All my kin wait inside for me to bring them word of your failure or to gape in shock as you enter the city to find the knowledge you desire. You, Stephen Lawson, must use whatever skills you possess to enter the hall, which, as you can see, stands open to you."

"It's open all right," Sofia protested. "But it's at least three hundred feet up in the air!"

The Black Ram did not reply. He steadily regarded Stephen as if expecting him to say something.

Instead Stephen thought of how Ivan had used his wits to win the Test of Strength, and how Sofia had used her strength to win the Test of Wit. In both cases, they had also used tools—Sofia, her new sword, and Ivan, the bottle of wind captured by his great-aunt.

They used the opposite quality to the one being tested. But what was the *opposite* of skill? And what kind of tool would let him fly up into the air?

He ran through a quick inventory of everything he had on him. Unlike Ivan, he only had the front and back pockets of his jeans, and there wasn't much in them. His phone—useless here and now—his notebook, and some chalk and charcoal for sketching.

"Of course!" he said.

He remembered when the tests had been first mentioned and how he'd actually *hoped* that he would be able to draw for the Test of Skill, because he was a skilled artist. Or a starting-to-be-skilled artist, at least. He looked around for something to draw on, and settled on a nearby stone block similar to the one that had been used in Ivan's test.

The magic he had inherited from his fae mother would let him animate his drawings. And she *had* said that someday he'd be able to detach his drawings from the surfaces he made them on as actual objects—like she'd done with the butterfly. She'd also said it could be dangerous and that it was too early for him to attempt it, but he glossed over that part.

He'd seen her do it. It *was* possible. He could at least try.

But what to draw? A knotted rope with a grappling hook so he could climb up to the hall? He'd never been particularly good at climbing in gym class, and that was an *awfully* long way to throw the hook anyway. He wondered if he drew an elevator, it could magically whisk him and the others up into the air. But that probably wouldn't work. The magical elevator that Stephen knew was a thinking, feeling entity—as much a person as any of them—and

Stephen didn't think it would ever be within his powers to conjure something like that. He thought of making a pair of wings like those in the Icarus story, but those wings hadn't turned out so well for  Icarus. He considered a jet pack.

Then the colorful walls of the hall caught his eye, and he decided what to draw.

Stephen reached up as high as he could and began sketching with a stick of charcoal in one hand and a piece of chalk in the other. He worked quickly, making a round shape with ropes stretching down to a square shape. The more details he drew in, the more obvious it became what he was drawing.

"A hot-air balloon!" said Ivan. "Ingenious!"

"What is a hot-air balloon?" asked Makh. "It looks dangerous."

"Some sort of conveyance for carrying humans through the air, obviously," said the Black Ram.

His drawing as complete as he could make it, Stephen stepped back. He saw a few imperfections, but his mother had also told him that perfection was impossible, even for fae artists, so he decided the piece was done. But now what to do? She'd just reached out and seemed to pull the butterfly from the wall.

He concentrated, holding his hands out and *willing* the balloon to detach itself from the stone block it was drawn upon. The balloon began to spin slowly, revealing details that Stephen hadn't drawn but only imagined. . . .

Yet it remained trapped on the surface of the stone.

Sweat beaded on his forehead. He thought as hard as he could. Why wasn't it working?

"It is not working because you do not yet possess sufficient magical power to pull an artistic creation fully into the realm of the real," said the Black Ram. There was an odd note in his voice. "Only the most powerful fae artists are able to work that magic, and you are very young."

And only half fae, thought Stephen, for the first time disappointed. He had been so sure that his skill at drawing would save the day, especially after Ivan and Sofia had done so well in their tests. He'd really believed the three of them together could do anything—even gain admittance into the Grove of Memory.

What else can I do? he wondered. *What* else *am I skilled at? Anything?*

Stephen didn't want to look at Sofia and Ivan, because he was afraid of what he'd see there: He was failing them. He alone would make them unable to pass the test.

"Stephen Lawson," Sofia said, "don't even think of giving up. You've got this."

He turned to them.

Ivan gave him a nod. "You cheered us on every step of our tests. None of them have been easy. I almost didn't make it through mine."

They were comforting him. Cheering for him.

Believing in him. Because they were his friends, and that was what friends did. And Stephen *had* done the same, because he was their friend, too.

Just like that, he had an inkling about something else he was skilled at. And maybe, right now, it was the most important skill to possess.

There was another sphinx besides the Black Ram, after all, who wasn't up in the floating Hall of Sand and Wind. The so-called Great Sphinx. The supernormal that had been turned to stone by a great betrayal—and Stephen understood—was the reason for all these barriers, all these tests. The sphinx people had stopped welcoming outsiders as friends because of Kindlefleur.

So maybe what he needed to do was convince the Black Ram that the three of them could be trusted, that they were friends.

Stephen had made more close friends in the few weeks since he and his dad had moved to New York than he'd ever had in his life. The elevator and the gargoyles; Cindermass; and his *best* friends, Ivan and Sofia . . .

Now he needed to make one more.

"What was his name?" Stephen asked, pointing to the massive stone sphinx.

He saw Ivan open his mouth to answer, but Stephen gave a slight shake of his head, and he closed it.

"I'm just wondering," Stephen said to the Black Ram, gazing between him and the stone sphinx. "Did you know him well?"

"He was known to us all," the sphinx said. "His name was Khafre. He was a great leader."

"What made him a great leader?" Stephen asked.

The Black Ram was silent for a moment.

Stephen waited for him to bark that Stephen should get back to work. To his relief, that wasn't what the Black Ram said.

"Things were different then. Our city sat on the earth, and we had many visitors. Khafre was sought as a source of much wisdom, and he was happy to dispense it. But he was too trusting."

"Kindlefleur," Stephen said, softly.

The Black Ram let out a muffled bleat. He was

still mourning. And angry. "Do not speak that name," the sphinx said.

"I know what it's like to lose someone you love and respect," Stephen said. "My grandmother passed away. She was a culinary alchemist in our time."

"I haven't met one of those in years," the Black Ram said.

"My dad's one, too," Stephen said. "I don't know what he'll do if we don't make it back to the future."

"He will go on, little one," the Black Ram said. "That is what we do when those we love are gone, isn't it? Now, are you finished? Your time is almost done, and I grow weary."

"I imagine you've been weary for a long time," Stephen said, stepping closer even as he saw Ivan and Sofia move back. "Kindlefleur is still hurting all of us. She's the reason we're here. Think about it. Dadelion made the ivory wand to force her confession. Then she hid it, because she knew that was a terrible power to have and never wanted to be tempted by it again." Stephen waved his hand at the floating city. "You stopped seeing outsiders unless they could pass your tests, and yet Edmund the Enchanter still used those as cover to sneak into the Grove of Memory."

The Black Ram let out a rumbling sound of displeasure. "He died here."

"No, he didn't. He stole the answer to Hakor's riddle. And then Hakor turned to stone, and my friend Ivan . . . Well, he grieves for Hakor like you grieve for your friend Khafre. Another sphinx friend trusted us to come here and bring back proof that Edmund cheated, and if we don't, then she'll be stone forever, too. Kindlefleur and people like her will continue to win."

The Black Ram studied Stephen, a thoughtful furrow between his eyes.

"We have come here as friends," Stephen said. "To do what friends do, which is help one another."

"I see what you've done, fae boy," the Black Ram said. "You told me what you wanted to discuss without passing the Test of Skill. Trickery."

Stephen studied his sneakers. He'd been almost sure this would work.

"No," Stephen said. "Being a good friend is a skill. That's the skill I'm using. It's for you to decide whether it means I pass the test."

The Black Ram gazed up at his city, at the open hall with its many lights. Stephen tried not to move.

Finally the Black Ram looked back at him. "As you surely know, we cannot warn Hakor, because to do so would violate the laws of nature and time. It is difficult for me to believe this Edmund visited the grove unknown to us, but given that he is a magic user, it is not impossible," he said gruffly. "Particularly since we assumed he had perished. The guardians only alert us when someone *enters* our territory."

Makh sighed. "And Edmund allowed himself to be buried in the sand during the Test of Strength. He must have used his magic to stay alive."

"He *could* have remained here, then," the Black Ram said, "as we would not have disturbed his remains. . . . But to enter the Hall of Sand and Wind itself? That would take some further trickery." He paused and shook his massive head. "While I do not trouble myself with *your* concerns, I would not want to lose another sphinx or put my people in future peril if it can be avoided." The Black Ram went quiet for a moment, and Stephen felt Sofia and Ivan come up on either side of him, taking his arms.

"You have passed the test," the Black Ram said. "The Grove of Memory will be able to show you what you seek; it records all that transpires within it. We will see if the proof you need is on offer. I do this for sphinxkind. No other reason."

"Okay," Stephen said. "Thank you."

"Stephen, you did it!" Sofia shouted, letting go only to bounce around and hug him.

"*We* did it," Stephen said. He and Ivan exchanged a nod. Makh put his paws up on Stephen's shoulders to get in on the celebration.

"Let us go to the Hall of Sand and Wind together," barked the Black Ram. "The sooner you get what you seek, the sooner you can depart."

CHAPTER TWENTY

They didn't go up to the floating city after all. The Hall of Sand and Wind came to them.

Stephen watched with wide eyes as it floated down and down and alighted on the clear patch of desert behind them. Sounds of cheers and the welcome smells of feasting traveled with it—the scent of roasting meat made Stephen's mouth water and his stomach growl. They hadn't eaten in almost a day.

Stephen, Ivan, and Sofia stayed close together as they entered the raucous hall. The tables were set with rows upon rows of food, and sphinxes with rams' heads and with people's faces and with falcons' beaks and feathers sat on the ground before them. Sphinx children peered at the friends curiously as they passed by.

"Outsiders are not permitted to join our feasts," the Black Ram said. "Follow me."

"We don't have time to eat anyway," Sofia said. Though Stephen suspected all three of them would devour the first food that came their way.

The Black Ram led them through the hall and to a wall of billowing curtains. The large chamber they passed into had walls of what looked to be stone, and yet must somehow be light enough or magical enough to fly through the air as needed.

The walls and ceiling were carved to resemble the sheets of canvas and silk that made up most of the city. The floor was sand, and felt as solid as the desert. But the chamber was crowded with thorny trees. Every tree had dozens of branches, and every branch had dozens of smaller, dangling branches.

"Welcome to the Grove of Memory," said the Black Ram, "a place held both sacred and secret by all of sphinxkind. You, time travelers, and you, Makh Canis, have been allowed here because you passed the tests and sought to aid one of our own. After the revelation that someone may have trespassed here, I vow that no other outsiders shall ever visit it again. We will see if you are correct. Nevertheless, our guardians shall now be on alert for *all* invaders. Welcome, last guests, to the place of answers, the place of keys."

Yes, Stephen realized. *Those aren't leaves and thorns growing from the branches—they are* keys. Long keys made of living wood, straight and thick with toothy formations along the edges.

A light breeze blew through the chamber at the Black Ram's words, and the keys all clattered against one another. They sparkled with light, revealing that almost every key was inscribed with mystical symbols. Words of some kind were deeply carved, and from what Stephen could see, seemingly on both sides of every key.

Ivan was looking around wide-eyed. "I've never seen or heard of anything like this place. It's beautiful."

And it was. Stephen was already planning the drawings he would make of this place, wondering what his mother would think of them.

"Are those names?" Stephen asked. "Do sphinxes come here and carve their names on the keys?"

The Black Ram snorted. "They are not names but riddles—riddles on one side, answers on the other, inscribed with our claws. Only someone present when each sphinx carved his or her riddle and answer would know which belongs to which sphinx. And the grove itself knows."

The Black Ram strode forward into the middle of the chamber. There was no obvious path between the tightly placed bushes and trees, but one seemed to appear before him as he walked, the branches bending aside to make way. Stephen, Sofia, Ivan, and Makh stood at the edge of the Grove of Memory, watching him for a moment, until the sphinx paused and glanced over his shoulder.

"Come," he said brusquely.

They filed after their host in a line, with Stephen taking the lead, and Makh bringing up the rear. Sofia's hand rested on the hilt of Mother, but he didn't think she was frightened of this place—just that a sword at her side was a comfort to her.

They reached the center of the chamber, where there was a small clearing in the grove. A low stone dais took up most of the space, and a large tree stump was at its center. They followed the sphinx to the stump and stood in a circle around it.

"This is the heart of the grove. All its memories live inside it. If Edmund the Enchanter was present when Hakor devised the answer to his riddle, then his presence was recorded," the Black Ram said.

"So, the grove is also a fancy surveillance system?" asked Stephen. "Like in stores?"

"I do not know most of those words," said the Black Ram. "But it keeps a record."

"Ah," Ivan interjected, "I think I understand. These trees maintain the memory of every act that takes place here. Once we leave, we'll be part of their memory, too." He pushed his glasses up on his nose. "Can they show us the event in question? Hakor carving his riddle?"

"Yes," said the Black Ram. "That is why your sphinx friend sent you here."

Sofia raised her hand. "Can we make a video of

what it shows us? We'll need actual proof."

The Black Ram rose up taller. "Knowledge has never left this place in any but the mind of a sphinx!"

Sofia didn't back down. "Bekhetamun said we would be able to get proof of what Edmund did—that he trespassed in the grove. Knowledge of proof isn't enough. We have to be able to, well, show it to other people."

The Black Ram paced around the stump, the trees around it swaying to allow him space.

"We need an answer," Stephen said. He took his phone from his pocket, but left it off. "We have to get back."

"Yes," Ivan said, pulling out his strange compass and consulting it. "Our travel to this time must end soon, or we will be too late."

"If you agree, we can record a video of what the grove has to show us and promise to let only the Octagon see it. We will erase it once this is finished," Stephen said, pleading with the sphinx.

The Black Ram stopped his pacing and considered the phone.

"I do not understand what this video record is," the Black Ram said.

"A visual memory," Ivan said. "Like the trees, but using technology. Technology is how the pyramids got built. It's using the science of the world, and not the magic. Oh wait, do I need to define—"

"Stop. We are not ignorant here." The Black Ram stood silent for a long moment. "Yes, as long as it does not require a connection with your present reality, this visual memory of yours should be possible. If your friend told you that proof was necessary, then I will allow it."

Stephen relaxed, until . . .

The Black Ram towered over them. "However, if you do not destroy this memory, there will be consequences. Sphinxes have long lives."

"Okay," Stephen said. "So what happens now?"

The Black Ram smiled, flashing his big broad teeth. It wasn't a pleasant sight.

"First, faeling," he said, "the grove must look into you."

"Wait!" cried Makh.

But even as the dog spoke, branches from nearby

trees extended toward them. Smooth wood wound itself around and around his body, holding him in place. Branches did the same to Ivan and Sofia.

"What's happening?" Stephen asked, but then a soft green light filled the whole world. The grove surrounding them was replaced by a new scene so convincing that Stephen almost thought he'd been teleported somewhere.

Green walls on each side of him; a walkway that split ahead. The floor was blue and the sky above was blue, too, scudded with thin wisps of white cloud. He looked down at his clothes. He still wore jeans and a T-shirt and sneakers, but yes, now they were all the same gemstone shade of blue. As was his skin. It had taken on a hue close to his mother's.

"Where am I? What's going on?" he shouted as loudly as he could. His voice echoed into the distance. There was no answer.

The walls were about twice as tall as Stephen was. He put his hand on one. It was smooth and cool to the touch. He took a few steps forward and came to an intersection.

"Okay, it's a maze. I know how to solve mazes."

The trick, his father had taught him when they'd visited a corn maze in the countryside on a day trip out of Chicago, was to always turn right *or* left, but never to mix them up. He kept his left hand on the wall and turned left. As long as his hand never lost contact, he would find his way through, eventually, either to the center of the maze or out of it altogether.

He took a turn and . . .

. . . was in his old bedroom in Chicago, drawing a picture of some football linemen arrayed across a field of blue. *But that's not right,* he thought. *Football fields are green, and I used green in this drawing I sent to Chef Nana.*

Then he was in the maze again. *What on earth was that?* he wondered. Some kind of memory, maybe?

He took another left . . .

. . . and there was a minotaur in a blue suit looming over him. "Be careful, boy," the minotaur said. "Not all who cross that fence come back." Which is what the minotaur at Chef Nana's funeral had told him, or almost. But hadn't his suit been black?

What had the Black Ram said? *The grove is looking into me. Is this another test?*

Another left, another memory. Another left, another memory. Stephen relived everything he'd gone through over the last month, bathed in shades of green and blue. Stephen decided that if he ever got out of this, he was definitely *not* telling Cindermass that he'd seen him as a *blue* dragon.

How long will this go on?

He took another left, ready for another slightly altered memory, but the maze had opened up. He had found its center.

And at the center was Hakor the sphinx, approaching a tree in the grove, murmuring to himself. Hakor began to slice into a key with his claws.

"Wait a second!" Stephen pushed against the branches still wrapped around him, but they were already releasing him. And there were Ivan and Sofia, the branches around them unwinding, too.

"We have to record this," Sofia said, staring at the image of Hakor projected in the air above the stump.

Edmund had to be coming. He *had* to. Stephen pressed his phone on, fidgeting while it booted up. Quickly, he turned the video recorder on and trained it on the scene unfolding in front of them.

Slowly, painstakingly, Hakor carved a riddle and an answer into either side of the key with his claws. The language was nothing Stephen could read.

After a long time, Hakor ran his claws lightly over both sides, and they glowed. The branches clicked in the wind, glowing all around him. And . . . he left.

"He's gone!" Stephen said, dismayed.

"Keep filming," Ivan said, a prayer in his voice.

The grove continued the scene in front of them, but Stephen couldn't see why. Edmund was nowhere in sight.

But then: "Something's happening!" Sofia said.

She was right. The branch in the center of the image, the one holding Hakor's key, dipped low. As if unseen fingers pulled it down. A pot of something purple appeared, and the key vanished into it.

The Black Ram growled. "Trickery! The Hall

lands each night only at my command. I would never allow it to touch the ground knowing invaders were present."

"It must have been Edmund," Ivan said. "He used some sort of invisibility cloak or spell. That's how he snuck in here! He knew when Hakor would be making his marks. He came to take the tests, faked his own death, and then waited until the hall touched down! He could've hidden inside as long as he had to, waiting for Hakor! It was a masterful plan."

The Black Ram growled again.

As they watched, the pot swirled, and then the key sprang up, the branch, rebounding, all as if nothing had happened. The pot vanished.

"He made a copy of the key!" Ivan said.

"He cheated," Stephen said, as the image began to fade. "That's what matters."

"But we can't see it was him," Sofia said.

"And neither will the Octagon," Ivan said, his voice shaking. "Edmund has outsmarted us again."

CHAPTER
TWENTY-ONE

The Black Ram waved a paw at the trees surrounding them. "The Grove of Memory has shown you what it can," he said. "What you do is up to you, but remember the promises you have made. Not just to me, but to the others of my kind."

"How could we ever forget?" Ivan said.

Stephen thought of stone Hakor and, beside him, stone Bek.

Sofia stepped up in front of them. "We have the video showing that someone was here after Hakor. Maybe if we get back in time, with the circumstantial evidence against Edmund, it'll be enough. But we should go."

"I will come with you," said Makh. "I may be of some use."

The Black Ram gazed down at the dog, who gazed right back at him. The Black Ram said, in his gruff way, "You are brave as well as loyal."

If the Black Ram didn't worry about Makh coming with them, Stephen supposed he shouldn't either.

"Thank you," Ivan said to the Black Ram. "For . . . trying to help us in the end. For everything."

To Stephen's amazement, the Black Ram winked one flashing eye at him. "Everything? Even the dunes?"

Ivan mulled this over. "Yes, even those. We leave this place and time knowing more about ourselves. I, for one, would never have counted on passing a test of strength."

"And we leave with new friends," Stephen put in. "Even if you won't call us that. Good luck to you and your people."

"Farewell," the Black Ram said. And as Stephen predicted, he didn't concede they were friends. "I should warn you that time in the Grove of Memory does not pass as normal. You may have lost more than what you expect. And remember your promise. The proof must be destroyed when you no longer need it."

Ivan had unwrapped his jacket and fished in its pockets. At last, he plucked the sundial out and squinted at it. Then he nodded. Stephen and Sofia crushed in close beside him, the three of them holding on to one another's arms.

"Now we go the opposite of the way we came here," Ivan said.

They began to walk in a clockwise circle, keeping their arms linked. Just as the circle was almost complete, Stephen felt a tug on his jeans and looked down to see Makh the dog had grabbed the fabric at his ankle between his teeth. Then they were traveling through time again, with spinning and wheeling stars shining around them.

Stephen squeezed his eyes shut and opened them only when he heard a low growl.

Makh's ears were back, and he crouched low to the ground.

They were back in the Cabinet of Wonders, and

a strong wind whipped around them. The Unseen Guardians. The Docent hovered above them.

"It's okay, Makh," said Sofia.

Ivan stepped forward and inclined his head at the Docent. "Greetings," he said. "We've returned. We can give this back now." He extended the sundial on cupped palms.

The Docent's eyes swept over all of them and landed on Makh. "You brought back a living creature? To the future?"

"They didn't bring me so much as I decided to come with them," the dog said defensively.

"Do you think Makh's being here can create a paradox?" Stephen asked.

"I am only a dog," said Makh. "What can a dog traveling from one time to another change that would harm the time line? All will be well."

"The Black Ram allowed it," Stephen said. "It'll probably be all right."

"Perhaps," the Docent said. It waved a filmy hand, and the sundial was lifted from Ivan's palms. Aided by the Unseen Guardians, it winged away across the long room. "Were you successful in your task?"

"Yes and no," Ivan said. "What day is it, and what time?"

"Why," the Docent said brightly, "you're right on time. King Edmund's coronation will take place in an hour on the rooftop of the Hotel New Harmonia, under the light of the crescent moon. Long may he reign!"

The Docent was under Edmund's spell, too, then. What were they going to do?

Ivan blinked at it, then said, "We'd best get there, then."

"Yes, let's go," Stephen said.

The Unseen Guardians wafted around them as they hurried from the Cabinet of Wonders. Once they were out in the library lobby, they stopped.

"This is bad," Ivan said.

"Understatement of the night," Stephen said.

"We traveled so far," Sofia said. "No one would have believed what we just pulled off—even ourselves. There must be something else we can do."

They'd gone all the way back to ancient Egypt, and even so, Edmund the Enchanter might get away with cheating *and* his evil plan. Bek and Hakor might not be saved. *No way we're letting that happen. We're not giving up yet.*

"Sofia's right," Stephen said. "We know that Edmund got the answer, but he must have had to decode it, right?"

Ivan blinked behind his glasses. Once, twice. He pressed them up on his nose. "You are correct. It was in the language of sphinxkind. He would have to have translated it. Which means he kept it at least for some time—maybe he still has it. He seems like the sort who'd assume he's too smart to be caught."

"A long shot," Stephen said. "Since so far he *has* been too smart. But—"

"But a long shot that's worth it," Sofia said. "He just moved into the hotel. He could have brought it. That would be incriminating, wouldn't it?"

"Yes," Ivan said, stroking his chin. "It would. That plus the recording we have would be enough."

Stephen said, "Home, then?"

"Home," Ivan said. "Ours *and* his."

Suddenly the fact that Edmund had already moved into the hotel wasn't so depressing. It might be the thing that saved the day—this was their last-ditch chance to make things right . . . or bow to King Edmund.

Without a word, they ran outside.

Even knowing both Hakor and Bek would still be stone didn't prepare Stephen to see them this way again—Bek's stone face was set in determined, sad lines, so different from the happy, bounding sphinx girl Stephen had first met. Hakor sat immense and noble and unmoving.

Amun lay between them, his paws crossed one over the other. He rose to his feet when he saw the three of them.

"Hey," Stephen said, "we need a ride, don't we?"

Ivan said, "Good thinking. Amun, can you take us to the hotel?"

Bek's cousin stayed put. "Why are you going there?"

"Because we need to prove Edmund cheated and

disrupt the spell," Stephen said, confused. "So Bek and Hakor can come back to life."

"You mean to sully the reputation of the great Edmund, preserver and protector of all supernormals?" Amun replied. He took two menacing steps forward.

Sofia immediately had Mother out in front of her. Makh took on a low, ready-to-leap stance beside her.

Amun growled.

"We don't have time for a sphinx-and-magichound fisticuffs," Ivan said.

"You're right. We'll go another way," Sofia said, agreeing. To Amun she said, "You are bound to hold your post anyway."

Then she raced to the curb of the busy street, yelling, "Taxi!" and following it with one of those fancy city whistles Stephen hadn't yet managed to master.

Ivan exchanged a look with Stephen as they trotted after her. "One of us will probably have better luck than Sofia, since she forgot she's waving around a sword."

"Or not," Stephen said.

He pointed, and they both started toward Sofia, where she stood holding open the back door of a waiting taxi. Makh jumped inside.

Amun called after them. "You'll never best the brilliant Edmund the Enchanter!"

The goateed taxi driver kept giving them odd looks, and Makh stayed quiet. Stephen didn't know if regular people would be able to hear Makh talking or not. Or, for that matter, if Makh would be able to understand anyone but them or people who spoke ancient languages.

"So, what's the plan of attack?" Stephen asked.

"We should have one," Sofia said. "Ivan?"

They both looked at him.

"We'll need to get into Edmund's room," said Ivan. "Which ironically, means we need the same thing Edmund needed."

"An evil plan?" Stephen asked.

"No," Ivan said. "We need a key."

"Mom's master pass key would work," Sofia said

doubtfully, "but she'll have that with her, and since she's already ensorcelled she'll never hand it over."

"And the only other keys are locked in the safe, on Julio's key ring, or with the guest themselves," added Ivan. "None of those will work."

"Maybe if we, I don't know, snuck in through the ventilation system?" Sofia asked.

"That only works in movies," said Ivan. "In real life, you'd have to be half my size and twice as agile as you are, Sofia, to worm your way through the ductwork like that."

"There's one other possibility," Sofia said, brightening. "Besides the concierge's office and security, one other hotel department maintains keys to all the rooms in the hotel." Stephen was stumped, but Sofia continued. "Housekeeping!" Then her smile turned to a look of concern.

"Exactly," said Ivan. "Housekeeping. Staffed by the least friendly, least helpful creatures in the hotel."

"Well, them and maintenance," said Stephen, thinking of the elevator's constant complaints about the gray-skinned, black-eyed gremlins responsible for lubricating its lift chains and otherwise keeping up the mechanical systems of the hotel.

"Are you kids sure you're all right?" the cabbie interrupted them. "Should I call your folks?"

"No, sir, no need to call," Stephen said. "They're at the hotel."

"All right, then," he said, frowning suspiciously in the rearview mirror at Makh lying curled across Stephen's and Ivan's laps.

In silent agreement, they kept quiet the rest of the way. Soon enough the car pulled up at the hotel's address. Stephen had a few dollars and so did Ivan— luckily it was enough to cover the fare.

"You kids be careful," the cabbie said.

"We intend to," Ivan said.

Which wasn't entirely true. Stephen walked alongside his friends, afraid of what they'd find waiting inside the lobby.

But . . . there was nothing. Nothing greeted them, except the lobby itself.

Absolutely empty and absolutely quiet.

"Where is everyone?" Stephen asked. "The clerks? The guests?"

"For that matter, where are my parents?" Sofia asked.

"They're almost certainly with everyone else," Ivan said grimly. "The Docent said the ceremony was on the rooftop. They'll be up there. Preparing to crown Edmund the Enchanter as king of all supernormal kind under the light of the rising crescent moon."

"Right." Sofia shook her head. "Okay. House-keeping will have the key to Edmund's suite, but they'll know something's up the second they see us. We never go to their office."

"It probably doesn't make any difference," said Ivan. "They're certainly all upstairs with the others getting brainwashed anyway."

"But that's good!" said Stephen. "If none of them are in their office, we can go find a key to Edmund's suite."

"If none of them are in their office, it'll be locked, too, and the only way in will be ductwork," Sofia said.

"Which won't work, because none of us are mon-keys," Ivan said.

The first noise they'd heard since they'd entered the lobby (other than their own voices) sounded then. A screech. Followed by rustling in the branches of one of the lobby's trees.

The three of them looked up just in time to see one of the actual monkeys lower itself by its tail. It hung upside down and grinned at them. It waved.

"Well," said Stephen. "There's an idea."

CHAPTER
TWENTY-TWO

"**What's** taking so long?" asked Stephen, breaking the silence in the utility room. They'd been waiting for what seemed like forever.

"Monkeys aren't known for their efficiency, but it'll be back," Ivan said.

"It'll want another reward," Sofia said, nodding agreement.

She pointed to the big tray of fruit sitting on a nearby workbench. Stephen had liberated the reward from the fridges in the empty kitchen.

Finally a scratching sound came from the open grille up by the ceiling, and the monkey climbed into the room. It was holding something behind its back.

"Good job, monkey!" said Stephen, excited. He held out his hand.

The monkey jumped down to land in front of him, still with one hand behind its back. It held out the other, nodding.

"Okay, okay," said Stephen. He plucked a mango from the fruit tray and gave it to the monkey. Instantly the monkey tossed something over to Stephen and climbed up on top of a tool cabinet, where it began messily eating the ripe fruit.

Stephen caught the thrown object. It was a feather duster.

"Well, that's clearly from the housekeeping office anyway," said Sofia. She took the feather duster and placed it in a pile on the floor with a roll of paper towels, a travel magazine, a magnifying glass it had taken *two* pieces of fruit to bribe away from the monkey, and a caboose from a toy train set. None of them knew where the monkey could have found that last item, but none of them much cared. They were running out of time.

"Are you sure you don't have something in your pockets that can shrink one of us down to monkey size?" Stephen asked Ivan. "Or maybe some kind of monkey-human phrase book that will help us explain exactly what we're looking for?"

Ivan said, "Again, no. Our mistake was in giving this cunning monkey a reward for those paper towels the first time it came back. Now it's just grabbing the first thing it sees in whatever room it breaks into and trading those items in for snacks. And we're giving them."

Sofia had clearly had enough. "Not anymore we're not." She leaped up onto the workbench, drawing her sword at the same time. She thrust it out, spearing the mango from the monkey's hands, then jumped lightly back to the floor.

The monkey howled, but Sofia stood her ground. "Listen up, monkey," she said. "Here's what's going to happen. You're going to go back to the room where you found that feather duster, and you're going to find the key cabinet and bring us every one of the gold-colored keys, do you hear me? And if you don't, you'll not get another piece of fruit."

The monkey grumbled, licking its fingers.

"And if you *do*," Stephen added, sweeping his

hand over the entire tray, "you'll get *all* the fruit."

The monkey grinned and then darted into the ventilation shaft.

The lock clicked. The knob turned. The three of them sighed in relief.

The monkey had brought them twenty-four gold-colored keys, one for each of the luxury suites on the upper floors. The one that finally opened Edmund's door was the seventeenth they'd tried.

"Okay, Stephen," asked Sofia. "Are you ready with your camera?"

"Yes," said Stephen, tapping the RECORD button on his phone.

"Ivan?" prompted Sofia.

"Ahem, yes," said Ivan. He turned to the camera. "This is Ivan La Doyt, along with my colleagues, Sofia Gutierrez and Stephen Lawson. We are preparing to enter the lair of the archcriminal Edmund the Enchanter, where we anticipate locating the final piece of evidence we need to prove, beyond any doubt, the nefarious nature of his recent deeds!"

Stephen asked, "That's a little much, don't you think? Should we start over?"

Sofia urged them on. "No time. Let's just get this done. Stephen, keep recording. Ivan, tone it down."

Like the floors of the hotel, the luxury suites were configured by the Manager to reflect the needs, tastes, and desires of the guests staying in them. Stephen had been in one used by his mother's adversaries from the realm of Faery that just looked like a fancy hotel room, and he'd been in another used by Count von Giertsen af Morgenstierne that had reflected an undead lord's idea of luxury: bubbling blood fountains, black velvet curtains, and a creepy old fireplace.

This suite looked like neither of those. It looked like, well, it looked kind of like Stephen's room in the cottage up on the roof.

Sure, Stephen's bookshelves didn't have the same moldering old leather-bound tomes, no doubt filled with ancient and forbidden knowledge, as Edmund's, but still. There were other shelves crammed with everything from models of robots, to—Stephen was surprised to see—some graphic novels. He scanned the titles.

"Hey, he reads *Elfquest*!" said Stephen.

Stephen panned his phone around the room. The bed was unmade, with pillows tossed all over the place, including onto the floor. There was one corner filled with shopping boxes and bags that seemed out of place.

An open book was placed facedown on the night-stand, and a room service cart holding a mess of empty dishes sat nearby. "Looks like he had Dad's famous flapjacks for breakfast," said Stephen.

"Spread out," said Sofia. "We've got to find the key."

Makh, who had been his usual quiet self to this point, trotted across the suite to an alcove next to a couch. There was a narrow table covered in various objects—Stephen saw some sort of spyglass on a stand, and smaller items he couldn't quite make out—and above it a piece of art.

"This," Makh said, "this is most extraordinary."

Ivan and Sofia moved in to examine the large framed sketch done in charcoal and pastels. Stephen stood behind them, filming.

Whoever had made the drawing had an excellent hand for portraiture, because there was no doubting who was depicted. Dadelion stood smiling out at the viewer, her hand on Bastet's shoulder. Bastet was looking at her, while at their feet, Makh chased a pair of kittens. The entire portrait vibrated with life; someone skilled in fae animation had drawn it. But . . .

"Did Edmund draw that?" Stephen asked. "Can he animate things?"

"There's a signature," said Makh. "But I cannot read your modern languages."

"Not Edmund," said Ivan, who leaned over the narrow table for a closer look. "He must have hired someone else to make the drawing from his description. This is just an initial, the letter A."

Sofia stepped aside, and Stephen moved in to see where Ivan was pointing. He recognized the handwriting. He should have, he realized, recognized the confident lines of the drawing and the way it moved.

Now that he did, the situation seemed even more dire.

"My mother drew this," he said.

Sofia gasped. His mother, a member of the Octagon, was under Edmund's sway. "Oh Stephen, I'm sorry."

"Mom said the Octagon had protections, but that they weren't infallible."

"But this shows there is good within him as well," Makh said. "It is a memento. To remind Edmund of friends he'd never see again. He misses us. I can only hope he misses the person he was *with* us."

"Except for the part where he tricked you," Stephen said.

"A mistake, to be sure," Makh said.

Stephen realized he'd let the camera drop to his side. He started to pan back up, but then recognized what was in the frame of his camera. "Hey, look at this."

It was the waxy purple key, hidden in plain

sight among the objects on the table.

"He didn't even bother to conceal it," Ivan said, plucking the copy of the key up and holding it as Stephen filmed. "Why would he? This is his domain. Friends, we've caught our villain."

"Maybe the elevator can give us an idea what to expect," Stephen said to Ivan and Sofia, pressing the call button for the elevator. "It wasn't affected the last time I rode it. Maybe it has some natural immunity to Edmund's mind control."

But he was worried. So worried he could barely think straight. What if they were too late for the proof to matter? Would they start bowing and scraping whenever Edmund asked them to?

Bing! The elevator doors opened.

"You're back!" the elevator cried. "And not a moment too soon! Actually almost a moment too late!" And then . . . the elevator made a noise Stephen had never heard from it before.

The elevator was *laughing*.

Stephen gave the others a wary look as they boarded.

Makh hesitated. "Is this conveyance safe?"

"It is," Sofia said, waving him on. "You'll be fine. It's like a cart that goes up and down."

"Why, you've brought a dog!" the elevator cried.

"This dog is one of Edmund's closest friends," Stephen said, in case the elevator planned to object.

"Well, then!" The doors zipped closed, and the elevator started up. "You'll be going to the roof! And not a moment to spare, as I said!"

It laughed *again*.

"What, ah, is happening up there?" Stephen asked casually.

"*I* am to be the official mode of transport for our new king—within the hotel of course!" the elevator said. "Oh, but I get ahead of myself. The answer to your question is that Edmund is becoming king! It feels like he already is. Oh, I envy you the sights you are about to see." It sighed, and Stephen felt comforted. The elevator he knew was still in there deep down. "His cloak will be particularly majestic in the moonlight."

Very deep down. The elevator stopped.

"We'll see you again soon," Stephen said.

"I know," the elevator chirped. "I can't wait! Good-bye, new dog friend!"

The doors slid open, and the three of them and Makh stepped out. The Village was lit with blazing torches, marking out a large circle with a crowd around one edge. They couldn't quite see what was happening inside it.

"Greetings and salutations!" Sigmund Dormouse lounged on a tiny reclining chair beside the elevator, drinking from a tinier frosted glass decorated with an even tinier paper umbrella. He blinked up at them. "Here at last! Thank goodness! Your parents will be happy about that. Hurry now, or you'll miss the coronation."

The lights from the city hid most of the stars in the sky, but the fingernail slice of moon was plainly visible. Until familiar large wings blocked it temporarily.

"Cindermass," Sofia said, "he hasn't flown free in ages! He could burn the whole city by accident!"

Cindermass laughed, a hearty noise booming in the sky, as he swooped around above them. Stephen couldn't help but lose his breath at the sight. He *had* captured the essence of Cindermass in flight in his portrait.

"I don't think he cares. Edmund seems to have made everyone as excited as he is," Ivan said. He removed his compass again. Squinting, he said, "We have precisely five minutes until the moon finishes rising. We'd better get going."

"Five minutes!" called out Sigmund Dormouse, and his voice carried. The crowd erupted in cheers.

"Why do I have the feeling none of this is a good sign?" Stephen asked Sofia and Ivan.

"Because it isn't," Sofia said, and Ivan agreed with a grim nod.

The three of them, followed closely by Makh, made their way across to the cheering crowd.

Sofia pulled ahead of Makh and the boys. She had one hand on Mother's hilt, and a gleam in her eye.

"Remember," Stephen said, "no matter what

happens, we're here to prove that Edmund cheated so that Hakor and Bek can be unpetrified."

"We're not likely to forget it," Ivan said. "At least I hope we aren't."

"And hopefully the Octagon can be brought back to themselves, despite the whammy," Stephen said.

His mother was strong; he knew that. *She'd* help make all this right. And—he hoped—she wouldn't be too angry with him for going back in time.

"Excuse us," Sofia said, parting the crowd of hotel employees. Stephen scanned the scene and caught his father's eye. His dad grinned and waved.

Whammied, then. There was no way a wave and a grin would be his dad's reaction when he'd been gone for a day—time traveling—otherwise.

Apparently everyone had been whammied. The members of the Octagon surrounded a chair with a long, high back in the center of the circle. The Darkfell uncle bent a knee beside it, and beamed at Edmund.

That's not a chair, Stephen corrected himself. *It's a throne.*

Edmund the Enchanter sat in it, wearing the smuggest of grins and an enormous jewel-encrusted crown. His black hair was pulled back into a ponytail, and his usual cloak flowed around his shoulders like a spill of bedazzled ink. He had Dadelion's ivory wand grasped loosely in his right hand.

"Why, it's the children," he said. "Wherever have you been?"

Ivan gave Stephen and Sofia a look, and they both nodded to him. He stepped forward. "We have been to the past and then to your suite. We have proof that you cheated to answer Hakor's riddle. Your plan is at an end, villain."

Stephen held up his phone in one hand, and the purple copy of Hakor's key in the other.

Edmund studied them, his gaze resting on each in turn. When his eyes got to Makh, he pulled back as if stung.

He diverted his attention back to the crowd. "Does anyone here care about this?" Edmund asked. Then added, "The correct answer is no."

"No, King Edmund, no," an immediate chorus rose up. A chorus composed of the eight voices of the Octagon.

"I thought not," he said. "You're too late, children."

CHAPTER TWENTY-THREE

"**Now**, if you'll join the crowd," Edmund said, lifting the wand. "Soon you'll be untroubled by such concerns—by *any* concerns. We are about to begin a time of great peace and prosperity for all."

"Wait!" Stephen said.

Stephen looked at his mother, who gazed back at him with concern in her eyes.

"Mom," he pleaded. "We've got *proof* that Edmund cheated! If the Octagon will just listen, he'll have to return the wand of Dadelion to the cabinet and put everything—and everyone—back to rights."

Edmund sniffed and said, "Dearest Aria, can't you control your son?"

"I'm terribly sorry, Lord Edmund," said Stephen's

mom. She was elbow to elbow with the bigfoot woman Roams on one side and the witch, Madame Veronika, on the other. "Stephen, you mustn't be rude to the King and Lord Protector. He sits on the Throne of Leadership."

So much for his mom helping them.

"There is no Throne of Leadership on the Octagon," Ivan said. "It's a council of equals."

"Yes," Edmund said, standing. "*They* are equals who are subservient to *me*."

Sofia put one hand on a hip. "You made up *another* title for yourself? Lord Protector?"

"Actually," said Edmund, "my dear friend Julio, your father, coined the term when he and all of his Perilous Guard bent their knees and acknowledged me as their leader."

"Thanks for the recognition, Lord Protector!" Julio called out from the crowd.

Sofia hung her head.

"Stephen, do as Edmund says," his dad called out. "Then we can have cake."

Beside Stephen's dad stood Tomas Chèvrevisage,

the faun sous chef, holding an elaborately decorated cake.

"You see, *all* of your parents are my friends and admirers now," Edmund said, grinning. "And it's time for you to join the party."

"Yes, yes," said Magister Otis, the mole man who had previously led the Octagon. "We're all the best of friends now—here, there, everywhere."

The formerly glowering firebird, Chenghiz, practically beamed at Edmund. "The Lord Protector has even brokered a treaty between the steppe eagles and the Gobi dragons! The whole supernormal world is benefitting from his inspired leadership! Hello, Cindermass!" he called up.

Cindermass swooped low and then sent a stream of fire into the sky. "Greetings, Chenghiz, dear friend!"

Something black and furry leaped across the circle to their feet. Madame Veronika's black tomcat, Jersey Pete. He stretched luxuriously, then wound himself between Makh's legs, arching his back and obviously begging for a scratch.

"You see," said Madame Veronika, "Jersey Pete would never deign to touch a dog before now. Truly, all of supernormal kind must rejoice. I was wrong about Edmund all along. We all were."

They were making it sound like Edmund's taking over the world was a *good* thing.

"We have to get through to them," Stephen said to Ivan and Sofia.

But Ivan was frowning. "The steppe eagles and the Gobi dragons have been hostile to each other for thousands of years," he said. "*No one* has ever been able to make them see sense and stop fighting before."

Sofia nodded. "Maybe we've been thinking about this the wrong way," she said slowly. "Maybe there's some good in at least listening to what he has to say."

Stephen turned and pointed at Edmund. "Stop making them feel that way! That's not them! It's you!"

"You see?" said Edmund, sitting down sideways and putting his feet up on the arm of his gaudy throne. "Your friends are coming around as the moon rises. Even your fae blood won't protect you from seeing the light. It didn't help your mother in the end, after all. Though she did hold out longer than all the others—I forgave her after she offered to make me a work of original art."

"I apologize again for my behavior," said Stephen's mom. "I was being foolish."

"You most certainly were," said the vampire, Count von Morgenstierne, with a fanged grimace. "You all should have acknowledged the King and Lord Protector's leadership immediately, as I did."

"Please," said the mermaid from behind Sir Aqueous Fin's bowl, speaking for the fish. "It was the undersea community who recognized King Edmund's right to rule first."

An argument broke out then among those around the circle, with each representative of the Octagon, saving only Stephen's mom, claiming that they had been the first to become friends with Edmund. They all seemed to think that stating their case the loudest would be the way to convince the others.

"This is hopeless," said Stephen, praying that

his friends' true feelings weren't completely gone. "How are we going to get them to listen to reason?"

"Two minutes!" called out Sigmund Dormouse, and the fighting stopped.

Stephen held his breath, and then a voice he recognized as Isaac the bookworm's cheered. "Two minutes, folks! Don't sleep on those cheers!"

As directed, the crowd broke into cheers and applause.

Two minutes until it was too late. Permanently.

"Do we really need to spend more time on this?" Ivan said. "We're all friends here."

"*We* are friends. You and me and Sofia," Stephen said. "But Edmund is *not* our friend. He's trying to force us to like him. I know you can remember that much. You have to try. I have the proof on my phone." He held it up, hoping it would jog their memories. "We worked so hard to get it."

Ivan's eyes narrowed at Stephen. "I have *changed* my mind, that's all."

"You don't want to save Hakor and Bek anymore? Your real friends?" Stephen asked, trying desperately to break through Edmund's spell.

Ivan blinked behind his glasses. Sofia unsheathed Mother, then pointed it at Stephen.

"Leave Ivan alone," Sofia said, and she advanced. Stephen took a step back to avoid getting speared by the sword. And another step.

And another.

The crowd parted.

Stephen took a last step back and then looked over his shoulder. The edge of the roof was right there.

Stephen couldn't believe this was happening. Edmund was winning. After everything they'd gone through to stop him . . . He'd turned them against one another.

"Sofia, no," Stephen begged. "Think about what you're doing."

Stephen's mother chimed in. "What's the meaning of all this? Stephen, can't you just be a good boy?"

The words stung, even though she wouldn't have said them if she wasn't under Edmund's control.

Stephen knew in his heart that Ivan and Sofia

would be horrified at their actions. Ivan would never willingly give up on bringing the sphinxes back to life. Sofia would never threaten her family or friends.

Two minutes, Sigmund had said what seemed like forever ago. How could Edmund turn Stephen's friends against him, when he must know how precious friendship was? After all, he had earned the respect and loyalty of Dadelion and of Makh. Makh, who had been staring silently at Edmund all this time while Edmund looked everywhere but in the dog's direction.

Wait . . . Was Stephen beginning to fall under Edmund's spell? No, he was just remembering what else Edmund was capable of.

"Edmund," Stephen said.

The enchanter raised his eyebrows. "Yes? Are you ready to pledge your loyalty? This all grows tiresome! We're here to celebrate."

"No," Stephen said. "*No.* I'm not ready. And if I do pledge my loyalty, it won't be real." He swept the hand holding the key around at the rooftop.

"None of these people professing to like you is real—well, except maybe Count von Giertsen af Morgenstierne, because he's a bad guy."

The vampire bared his fangs.

"You do not speak to me this way," Edmund said, raising the ivory wand.

"You did have real friends, you know," Stephen said. "When we got back to ancient Egypt, no one there wanted to believe you could do the things you're doing. Dadelion was so upset when she told us the story of that wand. She never wanted anyone else to use it. She had hoped it would be lost forever. She knew what it allows people to do is wrong."

"Dadelion . . ." But Edmund said nothing more.

"She and Bastet helped us after we convinced them you were different in this time. We met the little girl you helped heal, too. It seems like the only bad thing you did back there was cheating. And then you came back here and turned Hakor to stone. Makh came all the way here with us, because he believes you have good inside you. Didn't you, Makh?"

The dog spoke. "I do. This is far harder than watching you fail at the Black Ram's tests."

Edmund stared at Stephen as if he was afraid to look at Makh.

"Stop talking now, boy," Edmund said. "I've heard enough."

Stephen's tongue felt stiff and thick in his mouth. But he fought through it and managed to say, "Did you know that Bek trusted us to get the proof so much she let herself be turned to stone? All so that Hakor could live again. Wouldn't you like to have friends who'd do the same for you?"

"He does have those friends," Makh said quietly.

"You know that even if this works, *you'll* know you didn't earn it, right?" Stephen asked him.

"Please stop your endless talking," Edmund said.

"Yes, this is very disrespectful to King Edmund," Stephen's mother said. But there was a frown on her face when she said it, like she didn't understand what she was doing. Like she didn't *believe* what she was *saying*.

"Your family and maybe other people hurt you,"

Stephen said, "and now you're hurting people. That pain is real, not all this admiration you've conjured. Things mean more when they're real."

"Things mean more when you have them." Edmund's fingers flexed around the curving wand, and he held it up overhead. "Ivanos La Doyt?"

"Yes, King Edmund," Ivan said.

"Please help your friend take this *proof* he claims he has and cast it off the roof. Let's put an end to this."

Ivan nodded and then walked toward Stephen. He held out his hand.

"Ivan, please," Stephen said.

"Give it to him," Sofia ordered, the point of her sword touching Stephen's T-shirt.

He shoved the key into his pocket and took a tighter grip on the phone.

Sofia rolled her eyes and rapped his wrist sharply with the dull side of her blade. Stephen's hand opened, and in the split second the phone hung in the air, Sofia's sword flashed again, sending it flying.

"No!" Stephen shouted, lunging for the phone.

But as he caught it, his feet slipped from the roof's edge. Beneath him was only empty air.

But then there was Ivan's hand, wrapped around Stephen's wrist. And Sofia's. Together they hauled Stephen back onto the roof. The three of them held on to one another, keeping one another safe.

"I would never let you fall," Ivan said.

"*We* would never let you fall," Sofia said.

Stephen could barely speak. His breaths came shallowly. "I know."

Sofia shook her head, as if to clear it. Makh gazed up at her and said, "Remember what Dadelion said. That the only way to counter her wand is to destroy it."

Sofia blinked at her sword. "Dadelion didn't just give me this to use with the Black Ram. She gave me this for right now."

She held her sword up, and it glowed with a faint light. She vaulted across the roof in an acrobatic leap, landing in front of Edmund.

Edmund scrambled back, dropping the wand.

Sofia's blade came down on it, severing it in two.

CHAPTER TWENTY-FOUR

The sound of the wand breaking reverberated across the roof like a roll of thunder. For a moment a calm descended. Then came the tumult of the members of the Octagon returning to themselves.

Chenghiz the firebird spread his wings wide and flew to Edmund's now vacant throne. He knocked it over. Madame Veronika was on her feet, too, pointing a finger at Edmund. "Don't even think about running," she said.

Edmund apparently knew when he'd been defeated. He considered his feet as if they'd suddenly grown tremendously interesting.

Stephen's mother had her hand over her mouth in horror. "Oh, Stephen," she said, dropping it. "I'm so sorry. I didn't mean those things."

"Mom," he said, "I know."

Stephen's mother pulled him into a hug. "Mom," Stephen said, "really, it's okay, I know it was the wand."

"I'm so sorry," she said.

His dad came over. He looked at them, then glanced back at the fancy pastry in Tomas Chèvrevisage's hands. The faun dropped it unceremoniously to the roof.

Stephen's dad joined their hug. "What in the world was that?"

Sofia strode back to them and was instantly enfolded into a hug by her parents.

"You did it!" Stephen called over to her.

"*We* did it," Ivan said, pressing his glasses up on his nose. His parents each had a hand on his shoulder.

"Your friendship did it," Stephen's mother said. "I have told Stephen about the essence of things, and it seems to me that the three of you together are the very essence of friendship."

Stephen smiled at Ivan and Sofia, who beamed

back at him, and at each other. "Members of the Octagon," Stephen said. "We still have two sphinxes to unpetrify."

A clattering ruckus interrupted. Sigmund Dormouse could be heard shouting: "This is highly irregular! Please halt all discussion of official matters at once! Why did we leave the chambers of the Octagon?"

"We'll have order, please," Magister Otis announced, rather grumpily in Stephen's opinion. "Sigmund, we'll allow it this once, on this highly irregular day."

The rest of the Octagon gathered around them, and Stephen cued up the two videos on his phone and hit PLAY. As soon as they ended, he produced the copy of the key from his pocket and passed it to Ivan, who held it up and said, "As you saw, we found this in Edmund's room. Is it enough to prove the cheating?"

"All in agreement say aye," Magister Otis said.

The Octagon chorused its "aye"—even the vampire.

"Hakor of the Nile's riddle was answered by cheating, and thus, he may be unpetrified," Magister Otis declared.

Ivan pumped his fist. "Let's go wake him up!"

"And then he can wake up Bek!" Sofia added.

"The Octagon will need to be present," Magister Otis spoke. "So first we must deal out a punishment for Edmund the Enchanter's attempted coup."

Cindermass swooped down, and people scrambled out of his way as he landed. He put his head right next to Stephen. "I don't feel like myself," he said.

"You're probably exhausted!" Carmen rushed over with Julio behind her. "All that flying. Let's get you back to your lair. The Manager will see to the teleportation." She snapped her fingers, and a retinue of newly free-thinking hotel staffers shepherded Cindermass to a less crowded part of the roof.

Meanwhile, Edmund stood, head down, awaiting judgment. To Stephen's surprise, he wasn't alone. Makh was by his side.

"Makh!" Stephen said. "What are you doing?"

The dog inched closer to Edmund, so his flank rested against Edmund's leg. "I am standing beside my master. Never has a sorcerer been more in need of a familiar's guidance."

Jersey Pete, back at Madame Veronika's side, yowled in what sounded like agreement.

"You would stay with him even if he's banished?" Madame Veronika asked.

"Yes," Makh said. "But I have another idea, if it is within the Octagon's power to see it done. If they're *willing* to see it done. If Edmund himself is worthy."

"What is your idea, Makh?" Stephen asked.

"First, we must establish that Edmund is willing to change. I have known him to be a different person from the one anyone here knows. And I believe that person is the true Edmund. But does that Edmund exist in this time?" Makh finished, and waited for his old master's response.

Everyone was silent. Edmund still had his head down, but he angled it to meet Makh's eyes.

The dog nodded, and Edmund raised his head.

"What I did was wrong," Edmund said, cheeks tinted an embarrassed red. "I came up with my plan, and it was a brilliant plan—that much I was certain of. I learned so much in Egypt, but still I couldn't let go of the idea of carrying it out. I should have." He paused. "I should never have left my best friend behind."

"I concur," Makh said. "Which is why I followed you."

"I should also remove this," Edmund said, and took the crown off his head. Without it—or his feathered hat—he seemed smaller.

Makh spoke again. "If that is enough to convince you all that my master is worthy of a second chance, I propose that he uses his intellect to benefit the three children who brought me back to him. He could be their tutor, and they could tutor him in return."

Stephen's dad said, "Fat chance!"

But Madame Veronika raised one slender hand. "May I have the floor?" she asked.

"Certainly," Magister Otis said.

"Lady Diplomatis," Madame Veronika said to Carmen, "you would need to agree with this suggested punishment. All the parents would. But . . . I believe that Edmund is sincere. And it would allow him to be under close supervision."

"I don't know," Stephen's father said. "I don't really want Stephen around someone like him."

Makh the dog whined, and Stephen spoke up. "I think Edmund could benefit from it," he said. "Trust me, there's no chance we start wearing cloaks and taking over the world."

"Cloaks don't have any pockets," Ivan's mother agreed.

Ivan's dad, beside her, added, "We could try it on a temporary basis, and if the situation suits, make it permanent."

"An excellent compromise," Madame Veronika said. "Everyone?"

"Fine, we'll try it," Stephen's dad said, as the others signaled agreement.

"Edmund, I encourage you to make the most of this opportunity," Madame Veronika said. "I am sorry I wasn't kinder to you in school, even if it was because of a spell. Now you will have a fresh start, if you agree to this punishment."

"This punishment is staying here at the New Harmonia and tutoring these three children?" Edmund asked. "And Makh can remain as my assistant and familiar?"

"Yes," she said.

"I accept. With gratitude." This time when he

lowered his head, it was with respect and deference.

"Can we go awaken the sphinxes now?" Stephen asked, tugging at his mom's arm.

"Yes," Magister Otis said. "And return the halves of the wand to the Cabinet of Wonders for safe-keeping. Let us never speak of the events of today to outsiders. Others will believe only that Edmund the Enchanter experienced a brief spike of renown."

Madame Veronika nodded. "The manner in which the spell was broken will cause people to forget his influence. The truth will seem unbeliev-able to anyone not intimately involved with these events."

"Wait," Stephen said. "You mean *I* get to know a deep dark supernormal world secret?"

Magister Otis said, "It seems that way, yes."

"Cool," Stephen said, and heard his mother laugh.

They didn't travel by car or bus or the subway to get back to the New York Public Library. Instead they all went together through the Folds. "What is one more irregularity in a day of them?" Magister Otis had declared.

Traveling through the Folds was both like traveling through time with the sundial . . . and not.

Everyone in the large group—which consisted of all the Octagon members, Edmund the Enchanter, Makh, the La Doyts, the Gutierrezes, Stephen's dad, and Sofia, Ivan, and Stephen himself—walked in a loose knot at a measured pace. The billowing mists of the Folds moved in every direction, and there was nothing to indicate which way they were going or how far they had come. Only Madame Veronika seemed to know the correct path.

The mermaid carrying Sir Aqueous Fin's fishbowl walked beside Stephen, careful to not let any water slip out of the bowl.

"It is a shame that your grand adventure must be kept a secret," she said. "The whales would no doubt have composed one of their epic songs about it if they ever learned of it."

Stephen glanced at the bowl, but the little fish didn't seem to be paying him any attention. "Is that *you* talking or *him*?" he asked, indicating Sir Aqueous Fin of the Reefs.

"Oh, *he's* busy telepathically communing with both the Kraken—who bids you congratulations on your task—and the shoals of magical dolphins approaching Manhattan from the south, telling them they may return to their normal business. The greatest number of them ever assembled had been on their way here bearing many treasures of the deep to present to Edmund the Usurper."

Stephen imagined what the largest number of magical dolphins ever assembled must look like, and decided he wanted to see something like that someday. *I wonder if there are spells that let you breathe underwater....*

But all he said was, "Wow. I guess we really did save the supernormal world."

"You really did," said the mermaid. Then she nodded toward Madame Veronika. "Look, we have arrived."

The witch was spinning her arm in a circle like a softball pitcher winding up for a throw. A rift appeared in the mists of the Folds, and the light and noise spilling through it was instantly recognizable as a busy New York City street.

Ivan, who had been talking quietly with his parents, rushed ahead, leaping through the rift almost before it had grown large enough to accommodate him. Then it opened wide, and the whole group was standing outside the library.

Madame Veronika made another motion, and all the normal people crowding the sidewalk stopped moving. Even the traffic stopped. The only noises to be heard were the wind, and the trilling of birds.

Hakor and Bek, each still petrified, sat atop their respective plinths.

Bek's cousin Amun approached from the library steps, bowing deeply to the members of the Octagon when he was close. "The Docent just informed me that my time here is coming to a close. I hope that the reason for my return to my former duties is a happy one."

"It is!" shouted Ivan, who was more excited than Stephen had ever seen him. He turned to Madame

Veronika, "How do I unpetrify Hakor?"

The witch smiled. "The magic is already working, now that we've arrived. Look there! Go to your friend!"

Ivan didn't need to be told twice. Stephen and Sofia followed at his heels.

Hakor's stony fur and feathers rippled, and just as Ivan reached the sphinx, Hakor stood with a great cracking noise and roared in delight.

"Ivan!" he said when his roar had died away. "Is it you who have managed this? I thought I was doomed to be a statue forever!"

"It's a long story," said Ivan. "One I will now relate in some detail so that no questions will be necessary."

"Ivan!" said Sofia. "Don't forget about Bek!"

"Oh, yes!" said Ivan.

Hakor stood almost as still as when he'd been stone, and turned toward Bek. Stone Bek. He couldn't seem to speak and then: "But . . . what has happened to my young apprentice?"

"Bek let us answer a riddle correctly so we

could go back in time to help you," Ivan explained. "She said it was the only way. As you can tell by the presence of the entire Octagon and your own unpetrified state, Bek's sacrifice was not in vain. But you can use your mentorship power to turn her back now. Can't you?"

It hadn't occurred to Stephen that Bek might have been making that part up. He exchanged a worried glance with Sofia.

"She should not have done that," said Hakor. "I would not have approved. But . . . I am grateful nonetheless."

He bounded over to the smaller sphinx, stopping in front of her, and then exhaling a long breath at her. Within seconds, Bek was stretching, then bouncing. She threw her paws around Hakor immediately.

"I hope he doesn't yell at her," Stephen said.

"I cannot believe you risked yourself for me," Hakor said, pushing back from his apprentice. "I will try to be deserving of your sacrifice."

Bek crowed, "You already are! You're the best

mentor I could have!" She began flying in circles, back to being the irrepressible Bek they knew. "Stephen! Sofia! Ivan! You did it! I never doubted you for a second!"

Bek's faith in them had been absolute. Which was something, considering she must have known they'd have to pass the unpassable tests.

"The sphinxes are restored," said Magister Otis. "Now the Octagon will return the broken halves of the wand to the Cabinet. The rest of you may go about whatever business you surface dwellers typically get up to." The petite mole man turned on his heel and started up the library steps.

Before Stephen's mom joined the rest of the Octagon, she went over and hugged him again. "I'm very proud of you. Do you want to come over and finish your lesson this evening?"

"Yes! I'd like to finish our painting," said Stephen. Then as she turned to go, he said, "And Mom? Do you think for our next project we could paint a group portrait of me and Ivan and Sofia?"

"Of course! Where should we set it?" she asked.

He thought of the Grove of Memory and how beautiful it would look in a painting . . . All those shimmering keys. But then he remembered that the sphinxes liked their secrets, and that the three of them had promised not to share any more than necessary. He took his phone from his pocket and deleted the video from the grove, just as they'd promised the Black Ram.

"Maybe in front of the pyramids at Giza?" he asked.

His mother said, "That sounds perfect."

Madame Veronika lifted her hands, and the world around them sprang back into motion, into life.

CHAPTER TWENTY-FIVE

Thwack!

A red croquet ball arced across the lobby the next day as Stephen, Ivan, and Sofia entered from the street. It crashed onto the marble floor and was headed out the doors when Julio deftly bent down and caught it.

"Oh no!" said Carmen. "Not this again!"

By "this" Carmen clearly meant monkeys on the loose, madly playing croquet in the lobby, and "this" was precisely what was going on.

"Are there *more* of them than there were before?" asked Sofia, just before she dashed off with her dad to try to wrangle a monkey who was pulling umbrellas out of the stand next to the concierge's desk.

It was hard to say whether there were more

monkeys, but there were definitely a *lot* of monkeys in the lobby. They clambered over the furniture, climbed the trees, and swung from the chandelier. Some of them were indeed playing some crazy monkey version of croquet, but more of them were making other kinds of trouble. Members of the Perilous Guard chased them in every direction, and guests were dashing for the stairwells and the exit, trying every way possible to get out of the riot.

Every way but the elevator, Stephen saw, which was its own sort of riot, with a pair of gargoyles attempting to restack an enormous pile of parcels and boxes atop a bellhop trolley. They'd obviously been knocked over by the chattering monkey bouncing around the elevator's doors. Every time Art or Sollie put a box on the cart, the monkey knocked it back off.

"See here, you simian buffoon," cried the elevator. "You cavorting cretin! You, you, *monkey*, you!" The elevator was trying to close its doors to the lobby, but the way was blocked with spilled boxes.

Stephen gripped his own precious cargo tighter.

Ivan and Sofia had come with him to his mother's apartment to collect the painting they'd finished the night before.

Edmund the Enchanter appeared out of nowhere—so probably the stairwell—and walked semiconfidently over to Carmen. Makh trotted alongside him, nudging monkeys out of the way as they went.

Stephen raised his eyebrows to Ivan and Sofia, and they went in close to eavesdrop.

"I can't get into my suite," Edmund said. "And . . ." He frowned in the direction of the parcels. "Aren't those all mine? Why are those gargoyles taking my new things?"

Sofia's mom shot him a harried glance. "You bought all those on credit from stores all over town, so they're being returned," she said. "And you no longer have a suite at the New Harmonia."

"What?" Edmund sounded stunned. "But . . ."

"You'll be living in the hermit's cottage up in the Village with the rest of the staff."

"Oh," he said. "Okay. Good morning, children."

His cheeks were slightly pink.

He's blushing again, Stephen realized. *Still embarrassed.* It was a good sign.

"Hi, Edmund," Stephen said.

But he could hardly be heard over the renewed racket of the monkeys. Sofia's mother held up a finger, took out a silver whistle, and sounded a high, long note. Then she called, "Monkeys, go upstairs!"

But apparently the rebellious monkeys had decided to stop paying attention to the Knight Diplomatis, too, because . . . nothing happened.

Or rather, a lot happened. The monkey next to the elevator knocked *another* box onto the floor. A monkey swinging from the chandelier went somersaulting through the air, closely pursued by an also-somersaulting Sofia. And a croquet ball rolled out from somewhere, coming to a halt next to Makh.

"If I may," said the dog. "Edmund, you are familiar with the cantrip of vocal multiplication, I'm sure."

"Yes indeed," Edmund said. He made an intricate gesture with his fingers, then patted Makh on the head.

Makh said, quite firmly, "Such nonsense! Such a tumult of trouble! Monkeys, attend me at once."

Magnified by the spell, his voice boomed throughout the lobby.

Amazingly, the monkeys listened.

They all stopped whatever ruckus they were making and scampered over to Makh, jabbering monkey talk softly to one another and looking at him. They even lined up, sort of.

"Huh," Carmen said. "Thank you. They aren't allowed in the lobby."

And she bustled away as the monkeys awaited further instruction.

"Edmund, I suppose we'll be starting our lessons with you soon," Ivan said. "But yours with us start right now."

"Yes," Sofia said, giving the enchanter a smile so smug she might have stolen it off his face. "This way."

The monkeys and Makh followed them toward the elevator.

"Don't think for a moment that you're going to herd all that gang of miscreants aboard me!" cried the elevator. "It's bad enough I must carry that dog!"

"Of course not, Elevator," Stephen said. "I just wanted to bring you a present."

The elevator was quiet for a moment. "A present? What is it?"

"You know how you said you'd like to have a painting by me someday? I couldn't think of a better place for the first one my mom and I did together than on your walls. Would you like that?" He held up the covered canvas in his arms. "If it's okay, we can hang it for you now."

The elevator squealed with delight and then said, "I can think of no greater honor."

Stephen smiled and stepped forward. So did Ivan and Sofia. Ivan brought out a nail, and Sofia a hammer. Once they'd tapped it into the wall, Stephen took off the cloth covering and settled the canvas onto it.

"It's a view of the park from my mother's apartment," Stephen said.

"I've always wanted to see the park," the elevator said, and sighed happily.

They moved back into the lobby, and the elevator doors closed. "That," Ivan said, "was the lesson. In case you weren't sure."

"No," Edmund said, "I got it." Then he looked down at Makh. "Let's get these animals upstairs for the Knight Diplomatis."

Makh said, "Follow me," and without a hitch, led the troupe of monkeys into the stairwell as Edmund held the door. When the door closed, things had almost returned to normal.

"Excuse us!" said Sollie, pushing the cart stacked with boxes toward the door, wings beating furiously. "We have to get all this stuff back to where it belongs!"

The elevator doors reopened with a *bing*! "I forgot to ask if I could take you three anywhere. You can admire how the painting looks! I think it suits me very well!" it said.

"Maybe upstairs," Stephen said. "I'm still kind of exhausted."

"To be perfectly honest, so am I," said the elevator. "Do you have any idea how many trips up and down I've made with those gargoyles and their carts full of boxes? Any idea at all? No?"

Ivan and Sofia waited, raising their eyebrows at Stephen. The elevator was his to deal with.

"Well, do you?" the elevator said.

"Um, no, Elevator, how many?" Stephen asked.

"Eleven! Eleven trips!"

"At least we only need you to make one," Stephen said. "Upstairs."

"Can we play a game of croquet on the green?" Sofia said as they stepped onto the elevator.

"You *would* want to play croquet," Ivan said.

Stephen looked at his and his mother's painting, with its swaying trees and blue sky. He looked at his friends. He thought about the hotel and everyone in it, about all the things they'd gone through in the past few days.

"I'll play," he said.

Sofia raised an eyebrow at Ivan. The boy detective started to say something, but then he just smiled and nodded.

So they played outside.

EDMUND THE ENCHANTER'S SHOPPING LIST

Three custom, sequined cloaks from the Witch and Wizard Haberdashery

A wand for every occasion

Mysterious black hair dye

Four shirts in every way as lavish as the cloaks, in canary, crimson, emerald, and eggplant

Amulet of Confidence ("For Those Days When You're Feeling Less Than")

Amulet of Handsomeness, same

Candles, five scented with old spells, one with ocean sunrise

Frogs

Frog collars, personalized: Toady, Slimy, and Greeny

At least three legendary grimoires, first editions

Personalized stationery: "From the Cauldron of King Edmund Darkfell, the Enchanter, Lord Protector of All Supernormals Until the End of Time"

Golden frames for certificates of witch and wizardry achievement

Socks, black